PENGUIN BOOKS
SOULMATES

Kanchana Ugbabe was born in Chennai and educated in Australia. She is currently a professor at the University of Jos, Nigeria, and has participated in the Iowa International Writing Program.

Kanchana lives with her family in Jos and actively mentors young Nigerian writers. *Soulmates* is her first collection of short stories.

Soulmates

KANCHANA UGBABE

PENGUIN BOOKS

PENGUIN BOOKS

USA | Canada | UK | Ireland | Australia
New Zealand | India | South Africa | China

Penguin Books is part of the Penguin Random House group of companies
whose addresses can be found at global.penguinrandomhouse.com

Published by Penguin Random House India Pvt. Ltd
7th Floor, Infinity Tower C, DLF Cyber City,
Gurgaon 122 002, Haryana, India

First published in India by Penguin Books India 2011

Copyright © Kanchana Ugbabe 2011

10 9 8 7 6 5 4 3 2

ISBN 9780143067917

Typeset in Sabon MT by Eleven Arts, New Delhi
Printed at Repro India Ltd, Navi Mumbai

www.penguinbooksindia.com

To
My loving parents

CONTENTS

Acknowledgements ix

Soulmates 1

Testimonies 15

Blessing in Disguise 25

Golden Opportunities 37

Jaded Appetites 49

Legacies 63

Survivor 73

Greener Pastures 83

Borrowed Feathers 101

The White Rooster 111

Rescue-Remedy 123

Louise 139

Exile 149

ACKNOWLEDGEMENTS

This work of fiction derives from my experiences as an 'insider' and 'outsider' in Nigerian society, sometimes a total alien, at other times secure in the warmth of belonging. When the society you have adopted sees you as alien, the estrangement is doubly felt. Walking a tightrope between cultures, some women, in real life as in fiction, survive and acquire a comfortable momentum; others lose their balance and quit the test. Straddling two cultures is fraught with hazards, but is also immeasurably enriching.

Friends and family have contributed amply to seeing these stories in print. I owe a deep debt of gratitude to them all.

. . . To Daphne Atkinson for that initial push, to Kathy Bodnar for being an unfailing friend, to Nana Abarry for being my twin sister, to Jana Mazierska for cheerful encouragement, to Devi Singam for being patient and dependable, Louise Hill for spiritual guidance, Ellen Walley, Imani Brown, Tina Juryit, Tanure Ojaide, Astrid Clarke and Martha Adive for affirmation.

. . . To Emeritus Professor Ralph W. Elliott, my indebtedness goes beyond this volume of short stories. As 'Onkel Ralph', guide, advisor, mentor and friend over the years, his person, scholarship and affection have spurred me on.

. . . To my children Onche, Isaac, Padma and Zara for giving me a precious identity to cherish and live up to.

... To my husband and companion of thirty-five years, Aako Ugbabe, without whom this collection would not have taken form. I do not have the words to express the measure of his contribution to me as a person.

Kanchana Ugbabe
Jos, Nigeria
May 2009

soulmates

There was an inevitability about his departure. Just the way it was meant to be. It had only been a question of time. Not that it came at the end of some dramatic event or mind-boggling discovery. That would have suited his personality better. He would have spun out an excellent story from it for the next dinner party—a story about broken glass, bruised egos, insults and abuses. This was a quiet, uneventful exit, an anti-climax, a being-told-in-no-uncertain-terms that he had outstayed his friendly association with the family. Anita poured the tea out of the navy-blue enamel teapot and looked up to see Uncle Wahab outside the window, boarding his car, suitcase and all. There were no goodbyes.

Uncle Wahab lived in his car, a smart, white Toyota Camry with a hood that could be pushed back depending on the weather. It was as self-contained and as fully equipped as any holiday caravan, his clothes on hangers, books, magazines, cutlery and china, the toilet items, and finally his cat. It was a well-fed female cat with large green eyes and streaks of brown and white across her back. She sat beside him, her tail encircling her in a furry ball, and took long rides across the length and breadth of the country. Serendipity she was called.

He was neither a demanding man, Uncle Wahab, nor a difficult guest but it took Anita several years to sum him up. He created a stunning first impression wherever he went. He got noticed. People generally fell over each other to greet him, serve him, answer his calls and attend to his needs. He was always dressed in immaculate white *agbada*, the heavy embroidery starting at the neck and trailing gracefully over his shoulders and sleeves, with an embroidered cap to match. He was clean shaven, wore leather sandals in original designs and carried with him a leather fold-over purse which contained his driving licence and other documents, and his tinted sunglasses. His car keys dangled from an engraved, circular metal disc which said 'Gemini'. His *parfum d'homme* lingered long after he had left the room. He looked like a politician on the crest of a wave, the managing director of a flourishing oil company, a successful barrister, or a close friend of the military head of state. His speech confirmed your first impression of him.

Uncle Wahab was a highly educated man, thoroughly polished in his register and demeanour, well informed on every subject that might come up in conversation, with an unparalleled wit to top it all. He was a smooth talker. He usually started by saying something personal to flatter you, and you could not ever doubt his sincerity. The surprising thing about a man so irresistibly attractive and eligible was that he was a bachelor. You could imagine yourself his girlfriend, mistress, lover or partner, Anita said, but not his wife. He was not the marrying kind, she said, even though he was well into midlife.

Uncle Wahab was ahead of his time even as a fifth former in the 1960s. While the other boys in the missionary boarding school 'pressed' their old shorts by placing them under their pillows at night to iron out the creases, he wore fancy long trousers that looked as if they had just come from the drycleaners. He was the proud owner of an electric iron. While his friends were driven to distraction by the legs of the English mistress, Uncle Wahab, being mature for his age, had had sexual encounters with one or two of the teachers at school and sat smugly back with privileged information, watching the rest make fools of themselves. He was a class apart. He was neither the most brilliant nor the most hardworking in the class but he regularly found himself at the top, simply because you couldn't help being impressed with his maturity and sophistication; he was macho before the word got bandied about his circle of friends. At university, the students would pile into dangerously overcrowded buses and battered old taxis, while Uncle Wahab cruised around in his pale-green Opel Rekord. Heads turned and girls made feverish plans to hook him for a husband. The called him 'Tycoon'.

He made his entrance as a family friend into the household. Anita was so taken with him on his first visit that she invited him to Sunday lunch. She was in a flurry preparing for the august visitor—the pestle hit her on the head as she tried to pound the yam, and the hot yam spluttered from the mortar and scalded her. Everything went well in spite of it all. Uncle Wahab looked sporty that day in his blue track suit. He picked at the pounded yam and *egusi* stew with a fork; he was a small eater. He entertained the family with jokes fresh from the Golf Club. When Anita offered him a drink, he smiled impishly and said, 'Anything as long as it comes out of a green bottle.'

He was a businessman, Anita was told, a prosperous one obviously, she surmised, among the numerous men of that profession who drove in and out of government ministries in the daytime, and out of clubs and hotels at night. Occasionally she heard him discuss contracts and payments with her husband. He could be counted on to keep an evening pleasant. His anecdotes were outrageous but extremely funny. He got quite carried away when he fantasized about his women—the German girl he had made love to with the help of a dictionary, the African-American girl who had accompanied him to a bar on 52nd Street in Manhattan and had then produced a dagger from her innocent-looking suede handbag. Chicks he called them (with total disregard for political correctness), like they were a whole brood of identical, feathered creatures. He had a return ticket to Miami, somewhere in his car, he said, which he must try to use sometime. He picked up stories as he went along, embellished and exaggerated them and made them his own. He could turn the intimacy of your dining room into a classic anecdote for the club bar. There was spontaneity and absolute honesty about the way he delivered them—he got under your skin effortlessly. Women seemed to feature more in his conversation than in his life.

During one of his prolonged visits to the north, Uncle Wahab was a regular visitor at Anita's home. He was like a member of the family, really, only he didn't bring his suitcase upstairs. He booked into the Sheraton from time to time and became a member of the hotel family as well. He knew the waitresses by their first names, the bar was his personal lounge and the cook gave him a preview of the day's menu. Even the janitor saluted with familiarity at the sight of the Toyota Camry, gratefully accepting the fifty-naira note tucked in his palm.

Uncle Wahab seldom had his meals at the hotel. He preferred home cooking. Anita set a place for him at the table every day, beside her husband. After dinner, he and Anita's husband, Bayo, would go out for the evening. Bayo occasionally commented on his friend's tightfistedness, particularly when it came to women—the rows he had had with the local women—but the accounts didn't seem to match what Anita saw of Uncle Wahab. Mind you, he never brought anything, she said, not even a token gift, a packet of biscuits for the children or a bunch of bananas when he came to visit. He had on one occasion brought some mangoes into the house and had then sat down and eaten them all. But then it was not something you could hold against him. His flirtatious smile and otherwise gentle spirit made up for any deficiency.

It was the fasting period just before Ramadan. The market came alive with a riot of colours. Anita haggled with Aliyu the fruit seller as he tried to cash in on the season. He dusted his pineapples and sat them up on the enamel tray. The pale-green oranges were arranged according to size in pyramids, the blemishes facing the inside. The bananas sat fanned out, and glistened in the evening sun. Aliyu stood over this fare with an orange in the palm of his left hand, easing the top skin off it gently with a razor blade. Sometimes he would bring out his feather duster and dust his fruit. Towards late evening, he sprinkled water over them, sliced the pineapples and arranged them on a bed of curly orange peels on the enamel tray.

Anita set the fruit salad on the table. Bayo was on the prayer mat, saying his evening prayers. Uncle Wahab washed his feet outside, with water from the blue plastic kettle and prepared to break his fast. He had a new joke for the occasion. It was about a man and his wife in bed, watching a televangelist preaching his message after the late-night news. The preacher invited his audience with health disorders to touch (with faith) wherever it hurt most, while he prayed. At the end of the session there was promise of miraculous healing. The man grabbed his crotch. His wife looked at him and said, 'Don't be silly! The reverend is talking about healing the sick, not raising the dead!'

'I thought your mind would be pure, considering the season and all,' Anita said.

'May Allah forgive me,' Uncle Wahab replied with mock seriousness.

He was gone for months and the family had periodic phone calls from the Lagos Sheraton that he was negotiating a deal in the aircraft industry. He always surfaced at an extraordinary hour—11 p.m. or thereabouts, when the padlocks had been put on the gates, and the doors secured. He then stood, all in white like a phantom, white trousers, white embroidered kaftan and cap, white shoes—and the white Toyota Camry strategically parked to highlight the total effect. Anita, in her dressing gown rushed to the fridge for green bottles, and apologized profusely when there were none.

'Oh, that's all right,' he said with his usual charm, 'I drink only Guinness these days.'

That night they got into a lengthy argument about which were more erotic, Erica Jong's books or *Playboy* magazine. Uncle Wahab defended *Playboy* with the fiercest egotistical arguments. It was art, he said, not pornography. Erica Jong, on the other hand, turned him off, she was too surgical about sex. He talked of Hugh Hefner as if he were a long lost friend, and of renewing his membership with the Playboy club in London. Other big names were casually dropped in the course of the evening.

He had been stationed in India briefly during his period of training as a diplomat. The *Playboy* magazine addressed to him had arrived by post. The following day, Uncle Wahab was summoned for questioning by the officious local police chief. His reply was to produce a picture postcard of erotic temple carvings in south India.

'Which is pornographic?' he had asked the sub-inspector with oily hair leering at the topless female in the centrespread of the magazine. 'This, or my *Playboy*?'

'Very nice,' grinned the police chief, shaking his head in an irregular direction.

Anita got progressively more tired as Uncle Wahab split hairs and entered into midnight logic, spurred on by the White Horse whiskey at his side. She went to bed.

That night he implored Bayo to let him stay the night. The guest room was full of cobwebs, the bed hadn't been made but it was better than sleeping in a parked Toyota, with Serendipity the cat. When he stepped out the next day, all in white, who could tell he hadn't spent the night in the executive suite of the Sheraton?

The cracks in the plaster first showed when Bayo came home late from work one day, and said he had been at the police station trying to bail out Uncle Wahab. There had been a series of car thefts at the Sheraton over a period of six months. The Central Investigation Bureau had been contacted. Workers at the hotel were interrogated and a surveillance unit had been set up. At 6 a.m. one morning, the police zoomed in on Uncle Wahab and arrested him and the girl he was with as they drove into the hotel.

Anita was appalled. How could the police? In this country, you are guilty until proven innocent, she protested. The thought of Uncle Wahab in his white kaftan in a grimy police cell brought tears to her eyes. Don't doubt his integrity for a moment, she went on. You know he keeps late hours. Sometimes he is out all night and then drives into the hotel at sunrise and sleeps till midday. That is his way of life. He just happens to be one of those people whose mind works best at night. It is unfortunate . . .

With Bayo's help and his own connections, Uncle Wahab got out of the police case that time. He dusted the experience off his white kaftan like it had never happened. He went away for a while to live with an old acquaintance, a local traditional chief, in his palace. He accompanied the chief on his ceremonial duties, participated in his traditional outings, and was a self-appointed overseer of the chief's farms and property. The polygamous chief sent his quarrelsome wives to live in the town house as Uncle Wahab became his minion, a Gaveston to Edward II. It added to his charm, Anita said. He now carried a peacock-feather fan, sported coral beads, and a gold band encircled his Citizen watch. He seemed to know all about soil science, the fluctuations in the rainy season, and about growing maize and guinea corn.

By the end of the rainy season he was back in town minus the peacock feathers and coral beads. He looked considerably thinner and entirely listless. When he said he had been doing crossword puzzles out of the tabloid papers, Anita felt a surge of sympathy within her. He looked hungry and didn't refuse the tomato omelette she offered him.

'Have you been ill or something?' she enquired concerned.

'Not enough sleep,' he replied, 'and not enough to drink.'

Anita avoided the green bottles in the fridge and brought him a bottle of ginger ale instead. His kaftan, which was unfailingly bleached and starched, now looked somewhat unwashed and crumpled about him. Bayo was pleased to see him back.

Uncle Wahab had also resorted to writing for the local papers. With great ceremony he brought out of his bag an article he had written and showed it to Anita. It was something about the ideal society being one without the motor car. It came as a shock to Anita when she found out that Uncle Wahab had come in a taxi and that he had sold his car. 'Cash flow problem,' he explained vaguely, in typical business jargon.

After a few days of Anita's pampering, and outings with Bayo, Uncle Wahab's swagger and bravado returned. The *Economist* and *Financial Times* reappeared in the living room. And so did the green bottles. Uncle Wahab knew every detail in each survey in the business papers. He had the inordinate capacity to digest information and bring it up again for use, in a bovine sort of way, when needed. He borrowed Anita's books to read, and always made perceptive remarks when returning them.

He had a fresh dossier on his return, of stories concerning traditional rulers. When a traditional chief died, he said, in some parts of the country, the chief's first wife and several young men were buried alive with the body of the chief. The idea was that he would be served in the other world as he was in this. In those days it was the slaves attached to the chief, but nowadays any wayfarer or stranger in the territory got thrown in! Another story concerned the son of a chief who had taken it upon himself to bury his father's body in the dead of night because custom demanded that the successor to the chief cut out the heart of the dead man and eat it! Uncle Wahab didn't need much prompting. He had an uncanny knack for sinister stories to which he added a personal touch—the man in question was a friend or the woman in question an ex-lover.

His visit lasted longer that time and before Anita realized it had run into several months. She wasn't sure when the good times ended and the bad times began, but between the blurred edges of the harmattan and the rainy season, she watched Bayo and Uncle Wahab get into a tangle of messy friendships and unproductive business deals. Uncle Wahab's jokes soured on her—they were too well rehearsed. She wearied of his chauvinism and finesse. Her home was gradually turning into something of a 'beer parlour' and Bayo was into special brands of men's perfumes. Further Uncle Wahab had eased out whatever privacy there had been in her marriage. She and her husband discussed the day's happenings, they fretted over their financial problems, they made plans for the future, and they quarrelled and made up—all in Uncle Wahab's presence.

In the half light between night and dawn Bayo started the argument. 'How could you do that to my friend? You chased him out like a goat or a leper. He has done nothing . . .'

Anita couldn't explain Uncle Wahab's departure. Only a mounting chaos in her mind and an inability to cope.

'Can you lower your voice?' she said quietly. 'It's 4 o'clock in the morning. You're going to wake the children.'

'You listen to me . . . I am capable of any abomination on my own volition. I don't need Wahab to goad me into it,' Bayo convulsed with anger.

'But he gave you that seal of approval.'

'It's your imagination . . . Wahab is not perfect, but he is a friend.'

'Your friend . . .,' Anita started and swallowed. Among other things she thought of the imported toothpaste, the eau de cologne and the minty breath-freshener left on the dressing table in the guest bedroom. She hadn't intended that things should turn out this way but circumstances seemed to have a momentum of their own.

Uncle Wahab sat up till the early hours of the morning in front of the television set. He went through the Cosby shows, then Walt Disney's *The Little Mermaid*, and didn't seem to be very discriminating, though previously he would have dropped names of famous actors and directors in conversation. Now he took in anything that appeared on the screen as the hours kept ticking and the night wore on. At sunrise he crawled into bed in the hotel room with puffy eyelids and stayed there till late afternoon.

'I have always wanted to wear an eye-patch,' he had said to Anita once. He had a bee sting above his left eye, he said, and that meant he had to wear his photochromatic sunglasses indoors for several days.

testimonies

On most mornings the sun shines bright, and the fragrance from the jasmine bush wafts into my kitchen as I ruminate over my spiritual life, third cup of coffee in hand and Bible on the breakfast bar. I feel about twenty-five (never mind the menopausal symptoms), full of hope and excitement like there is so much ahead of me. It is the Gemini in me, eternally restless, perpetually needing something new, getting exhilarated over things otherwise inconsequential, expecting a lot, anticipating delectable surprises around every bend. In my mind I write the 'Dedication', and acknowledge indebtedness even before the book gets written. Beginnings and endings are interchanged.

Sometimes though, I wake up clumsy, absent-minded, vacant and careless in my movements. This morning I stumble into the dining room and drop my favourite sugar-bowl, which smashes to bits instantly. It is funny how I don't feel any regret or sense of loss. A numbness has crept over me. I feel that way about things now that are lost, changed and cannot be had again. That life must evolve, feelings must change and that favourite possessions fall and break is beginning to make sense. Possessions mean little to me these days. That exquisite, hexagonal grey pottery bowl with blue streaks will be replaced by something cheap and functional from the market. And ugly. I get out the dustpan and sweep the pottery pieces into the bin. Everything has its time and place.

I was not consciously dwelling on Comfort's testimony but something about what she had said the previous evening lingered in my mind with a certain insistence. Karen loved testimonies, and was the coordinator of our group that met on Friday afternoons at her place. Our testimonies were gold medals, awards for outstanding achievement which we sported on special occasions or when we had a visitor in our midst. I hadn't come prepared for a testimony, cleansed and sanitized, but Karen had turned to me suddenly and said, 'Can you go first?'

Testimony, a presumptuous word, implied change, that somehow in the scheme of things you had been bad but had now changed and the change had been dramatic. My life didn't seem to present itself in tidy logbook columns. The good, bad and intolerable in me overlapped in recurring patterns. So I was vague and evasive and talked about new experiences intersecting crucial points in my life. Loretta said she had meaningful scripture verses literally 'given' to her. She had opened her scriptures at random one day, only to find them staring at her in Word Perfect Bold. From then on everything had fallen in place and the meaningless mass of her life had acquired a purpose and direction. Jennifer had given up alcohol, parties and plunging necklines for a New Life. Vicky had had prayers answered with such promptness—the lucrative company job had been offered to her on a silver platter, which showed that God cared and wished to make a definite point. It was then Comfort's turn.

Comfort was a newcomer in our midst. Her husband had

been transferred to our little town from Lagos where she had led an active and productive life. She found her way into our group, seemingly out of boredom, and looked so contented, as if Friday afternoons slaked years of thirst she had had for the Word. The rest of us were prone to becoming personal and even volatile every now and then. Comfort neutralized our participation by saying something completely general and noble, or she stared at us out of expressionless eyes buried in her fleshy cheeks. I had expected something suitably evasive from her that afternoon as she adjusted the *gelle* over her head and assumed the posture of an actress about to make her debut on stage.

But Comfort's testimony came as a total surprise. 'I was bad,' she trembled. 'I used to sin all the time. But each time God forgave me. My mother would say, what's wrong with you? You're sinning all the time.'

She stifled a sob and dabbed a lace handkerchief over her eyes. 'Then my husband, he made me kneel before the priest and confess all my sins. That is when I knew how bad I was.' Several of us wept with Comfort. The thought of Comfort sinning made me cry. She looked perpetually doughy and pure, pastry-pure, and totally incapable of being bad. Veronica, yes—although we hadn't got to her testimony yet. Veronica had a streak of wickedness in her that came through even in her prayers. The way she moved those lusty lips, the way she made her voice sound husky and hoarse in turn, pouting as she did so. The words 'bad' and 'sin' matched her past and present, but not Comfort, distant and innocuous, and still using the Thees and Thous from the King James Version.

It was at one of these coffee mornings at Aunt Naomi's that I was drawn into Comfort's orbit. She sat in her baby-pink *buba* and wrapper with a bit of a slouch, one leg thrown over the other, exposing her ebony ankle with a silver anklet around it. The coral earrings dangled down on her shoulders and almost touched the gold chain that peeped in and out of the folds of the pink *gelle*.

'Have you read Psalm 27?' she asked, in our general direction. 'The Lord is your strength and your salvation. That is what the rocks in this town remind me of. The Lord's strength.'

'So what did they take?' asked Aunt Naomi full of concern, picking up the story that had preceded my visit, unable to contain the curiosity in her voice.

'Everything, sha,' Comfort replied, doughy faced and without a flicker of emotion.

'Jewels and everything?' Aunty Naomi pressed. Her glance riveted from Comfort's neck to her bare wrists, smooth and rounded, formerly burdened with twelve bangles of 22-karat gold.

'One man was holding me at the back. The other man took off my earrings. So gently. Both earrings, sha. And then he put his hand on my neck, like this, and removed the chain over my head.'

Aunty Naomi looked visibly disturbed as she pictured Comfort's shoulders being fondled by the man, his fingers caressing her shell-shaped ears, gently freeing them of the gold screws and clasps.

'And the bangles,' Comfort continued. 'You know he held me like this and tried to take them off but they were too tight. So I took them off myself.'

'We thank God,' Aunt Naomi heaved a sigh. 'We thank God for the strength He gave you.'

'I didn't even know what was happening, you know. The children were eating in front of the television. One man had a mask like this. He pointed a gun at me and said, "Where's the money?" The television was on, you know. *Dynasty*, my favourite programme . . .'

'Did they come in a car?' Aunt Naomi interrupted.

'No! Crystal Carrington had just had a miscarriage—no, I think they came over the wall . . . I didn't know what they were saying . . . The programme was so interesting. Psalm 86. That's my best. The Lord destroys your enemies. I heard them banging my husband's iron safe. They took his money and the CD player.'

'You see God's hand in all situations. What about the wrappers?'

'They took my Dutch wax, all of them and the George, the lace and the *bou-bou* from Senegal which I had just got back from the drycleaners . . . God is wonderful. I'm glad they didn't ask me to take off the embroidered kaftan I was wearing. They even fired a shot as they went out.'

Comfort was calm and unperturbed. She had a Bible verse for every occasion and plenty of gold left on her person for further visits by armed robbers.

It was Comfort who gave me an acute sense of 'sin'. Under her influence my mind became a video camera. Everything I said and did got replayed over and over in my waking and sleeping moments as on a giant movie screen, every emotion, every detail. It was frightening as I lived each experience ten times over in my mind. We were on the Scripture trail, sending the children off to school and purging ourselves in devotional groups that differed in tone and colour as the rich brown of the harmattan and the pasture green of the

21

rainy season. Sometimes I walked into a roomful of snuffles, women blowing their noses into handkerchiefs and scented tissue paper. They whispered and implored the Lord to hear their prayers and then thanked Him because they knew He had already heard and answered them. They reasoned with an invisible God—one of them got hysterical from time to time. If it weren't God she was talking to, she would have stamped her spiritual foot! Another melted at the mention of God's love and then quickly regained her composure. The third prayed like a headmistress, full of authority. The tone was even, the enunciation perfect. The words came without hesitation, either from divine inspiration or from years of practice. I sat on the edge of my chair, mute in amazement, trying not to miss any part of this hour-long drama. I opened my eyes a tiny slit to see who it was that cried so readily and frequently. They all did, including Comfort. They were moved so easily. What did they do when real trouble was at their doorstep?

There were times when the Devotional Hour became a catalogue of middle-class woes. This woman's husband had had a heart bypass surgery, the other woman had twisted her ankle on the golf course, the third had a child who was a slow learner, the fourth, a husband who didn't go to church. Every ailment got advertised and embellished by the community in the process of making it a prayer item. Everyone got burdened with the other's misery as we wept, drank tea, passed the cake around and wept some more over prayers.

Back in my kitchen, I rolled out the pastry, trying to get a reasonable-looking circle, thinning it out from the middle to the edges as thoughts rushed to my head. Comfort's tear-stained moon-face and testimony disturbed me. Why had she not given any hint of the spiritual battle raging within her?

Her husband was a jolly Father Christmas, taking in strays, giving out cash, gifts and donations to every philanthropic cause. She had a cook, a maid for each of her three children, and a chauffeur who opened the car door for her and carried her shopping in. What was the 'sinning' all about?

It was not our day for the devotional routine. I drove over fallen jacaranda blooms into Comfort's compound at midday. The dogs lay panting in the heat. Everything was still except for Comfort's voice in the living room, which arrested and stopped me in my tracks as I got out of the car. One of the maids stood against the wall as Comfort shrieked above her, slapping her in turns. I stepped on to the veranda. Father Christmas held a shotgun with which he prodded the maid. 'I'll call the police!' he shouted menacingly. It took me a while to realize that it was something to do with missing plastic buckets and teaspoons. The maid flinched with each slap and repeated her denial. The next moment, the smooth and fair underside of Comfort's foot landed on the maid's stomach as Comfort continued to pound her with her fists. The maid tried to support herself but fell in a heap as Comfort picked up a wire fly-swatter and hit her across the ear. The children participated gleefully in this jungle justice.

The human countenance is a marvellous work of art. The satin smooth facial skin covers all conflicts wrenching at the brain. The eyes are two clear, liquid and tranquil pools without ripples. Comfort's hands were locked together in devotion, *gelle* draped over her head in pious beatitude. We moulded and shaped our gods in our own likeness, and when we sinned, God understood and forgave us readily. Each of us had our individual reason for being there, each having little to do with God. It soothed us to hear that others sinned too

23

but it did little to stop us from sinning. Our testimonies were cloaks of self-righteousness—if we had been out in the cold before, barbarians untouched by grace, we were now members of the elect, armed with prayers and praises, looking with disdain on the uninitiated. Our world narrowed in dimension as every aspect of it got stripped down to simple good and evil. Devils and demons got landed with the blame for our weaknesses and failings. Occasionally we identified the devils in people around us.

'I have something very important to say,' Comfort began. I looked away from her at the bougainvillea in bloom outside the window as I wondered what form this confession was going to take. Would she admit to violence or would it be attributed to machinations of the devil? Would she call it sin or was she merely overcome by emotion? How would the group react to her disclosure?

'The Lord redeems the soul of his servants,' she continued, quoting from the Psalms, 'and none of them that trust in Him shall be desolate. You see, some of my kitchenware went missing from our compound on Tuesday. I have been so worried. I hate losing things, it made me feel so helpless. And then . . . Praise God, they were miraculously recovered yesterday.'

I remained silent as the group joined Comfort in a chorus of praise.

blessing in disguise

We sat on steel chairs at the outdoor village-wedding and ate crunchy garden-eggs dipped in peanut paste. It was delicious and we were starving. Here were the working and making of tradition.

After we, in our wedding gear, were ceremoniously seated we were dislodged and asked to make our entry, accompanied by the traditional drummers and video cameras. The sixty-year-old chief, my husband of thirty-three years and the man of the day, was in his element. His coral beads swayed, his pot-belly bounced, he undid and retied the knot on his pyjama cords, and with great dignity took giant strides into the bride's compound. His best man was a wispy little chief in a copper sulphate blue *agbada* and a red cap, who had to take several mincing steps to keep up with the bridegroom. We sat ourselves down again on the steel chairs. The compound was full of people, sitting, standing and spilling out of windows and verandas.

'Give us the fags,' I said to Jean and lit up no sooner had we sat down. Jean looked uncertain of her role on this occasion. What do you call a friend of the first wife—prop, staff, hand-holder, fellow-sufferer? The palm trees towered over us. In the clearing, canopies had been erected. Under one of the shelters, the Jesus Power Band from the local Catholic church had set up shop. A suave young man in tight pants convulsed holding the microphone. His female companions swung their backsides in unison as they sang Christian lyrics set to pop tunes. The sheer volume of the music radiated heat. Sweat dripped down our faces, necks and legs. I spotted a stack of plastic souvenir plates nearby and picked one up to fan myself with.

The chiefs in a canopy across from us began making the speeches, addressing the bridegroom with all his titles, honorary and earned—engineer, doctor, chief—his latest accomplishment being the taking on of a second wife. Kola nuts and money changed hands. The man with the video camera on his shoulder zoomed in on us and said, pointing the microphone towards me, 'How do you find all this . . . the traditional wedding?'

'Very interesting,' I said with perfect innocence, sounding completely uninvolved. More peanut paste and garden eggs passed by us in trays within our reach. We dug into them and opened up our bottles of warm beer. The women in the shelters across from us looked aghast.

In the expatriate café in town, the women had been hysterical. Home-made jam and marmalade in glass jars sat on the shelves, and pasta in cellophane packs. Enveloped in a cloud of cigarette smoke, they were raucous in their disapproval.

'The man is wicked,' Ellen began, foaming at the mouth, 'It is a breach of contract.'

'It is quite disgusting,' Regina added, 'I'll strangle him if I see him and hand him over to the police.'

'If only we knew then, what we know now . . .,' said Sarah, implying that it was all a question of wisdom and the acquiring of it. Except that one always became wiser when it was too late.

'My Vincent is an exception,' said Eugenia, 'but if he ever did something like this, it would kill me.'

'You'll see this as a blessing in disguise. Time to leave and go back to where you belong.'

'This has taught us all a lesson. We have to be prepared.'

'You can prepare nothing. You'll be like the proverbial donkey going from one haystack to the next and eating nothing—starved.'

The MC announced over the microphone that Blessing, or Chika the young bride, would now make her appearance. I adjusted the *aso oke* on my sweaty shoulder and lit up another cigarette. Lace and beads, gold and silver threads, and mirrors crackled in the heat of noon as Blessing emerged from the interior of the house, followed by eight bridesmaids in orange wrappers and blouses with butterfly sleeves, their skinny feet in enormous platform shoes kicking the dust. They were like a band of Amazons out on a rampage.

'She doesn't look happy,' Jean commented.

Blessing was tall and lanky, of dull complexion (yellow, as the Igbos say), gap-toothed, with a hoarse, cracked voice. Not a bluebell from the woodland shade, I concluded. Apart from her dazzling accoutrements, she had worn no make up, and her eyes looked weary with sleep. If it weren't for the fact that she led the band of Amazons, we surely wouldn't have known she was the bride. Where a bridal radiance should have been, there was fatigue. Her jerry-coiled hair hung untidily about her temples, crowned by a jewel-encrusted head-tie elaborately fanned out behind her head. Blessing looked like she had brewed the beer, tapped the palm wine and cooked the wedding feast before climbing into her outfit.

'Thank God it's happening now when I'm alive and kicking and not later when I might be decrepit and hobbling along,' I said. 'He would have left me in a corner and got on with it.'

'Do you think she's pregnant?' Jean asked, sizing up Blessing.

'It wouldn't surprise me—she'd be out of the door if there is no bouncing baby boy in no less than nine months.'

Blessing led the band of clodhoppers to the oldest chief in the gathering. He welcomed her, uttered a long-winded Igbo prayer entreating God to give her ten sons and an equal number of daughters, poured wine into a carved wooden goblet and offered it to her. Cup in hand, Blessing and her giggling train were off again, dancing their way through the crowd to the accompaniment of frenzied drums.

In the meanwhile, Benson, the chief, my husband and Blessing's bridegroom looked preoccupied with the impending weight of two families on his shoulders. He clutched his plastic bag of money, gave instructions, accepted felicitations and reluctantly counted out money whenever it was asked for.

At fifty-two, I am at the age when one is free of the menace of being a women—I've arrived at menopause. It is also as if with a double click of a computer mouse, I've faded into a kind of neuter gender. This is not the age for competition, says my husband, stripping me further of all womanly emotions, trying to convince me of the demands of tradition. This was not the outcome of a relationship; this was an arrangement, a way out of a sticky situation. *We* are marrying a wife, he says, you and me. He makes it sound like buying a deep freezer, another joint venture. He says I look tired and worried constantly. This is the age for bags under one's eyes, and of insomnia.

The drumming had put Blessing in the mood. The bride now 'searched' for her husband-to-be amidst the crowd, her bridal train in orange, clapping after her. Her friends cheered, the relatives teased, the dancing got more ecstatic and the drummers, delirious. The church band raised its volume and joined in the mayhem. Jean and I fanned ourselves frantically with anything we could lay our hands on—wedding programmes, souvenir almanacs. The mock search drew to a climax with Blessing finding her suitor-chief stifling a yawn and counting his money.

Smiling at us shyly, she knelt at the chief's feet and offered him the cup. Benson took a hasty sip, distractedly, ensuring at the same time that the goat had been tethered securely and the trunk of clothes for the bride brought in from the car. Blessing drank from the cup demurely and offered it to him again. The four mutual sips from the same cup sealed their bond as husband and wife. She and I had now become co-wives, co-conspirators in the game. Jean and I nudged each other.

Geraniums have grown in my baby-bottle sterilizing unit. The children have long since left home for distant lands. What I have ahead of me is not companionship as I know it but a sweet domestic picture of a threesome in front of the fireplace.

The souvenir almanacs were distributed to the wedding guests. In it, my husband the chief sits in an armchair in his lace *agbada* and gold-embroidered cap, shoulders slumped, coral beads about his neck. Can't wait to get this thing done with and have the almanac out of the way. Blessing on the other hand looks resplendent. It is her first marriage after all. The same butterfly head-tie, organza blouse that exaggerates her shape and size, and lace wrapper. One hand is on her hip and the other thrown around Benson's shoulder as she bends down in full ownership of the man. A picture for two, a composition that excludes me.

My fractured memories spill out of golden notebooks. Dead people cease to have ever existed in my husband's culture. As a child, he said, he and his siblings went through the photograph album and put huge check marks on the faces of dead people. Sometimes they wrote RIP on their faces. None of them knew what RIP stood for except that they had seen it on the tombstones of missionaries.

Benson—the name for a poor-quality wrist-watch in some Third World country. His betrayal is couched in language that defies doubt or argument. The sincerity of his intentions could never be called into question. The family feud over landed property could only be resolved by marrying an Igbo wife, a pawn who could be used to secure his heritage. 'If I had any other way of dealing with the circumstances, I would,' was his refrain. Testing the mood of the moment, he would sometimes add, 'It is war—I can't fight the battle alone.'

My heart flutters with unknown, unnamed anxieties, halfway between resistance and guilt. The Igbo women in the neighbourhood tell me what they think I want to hear. 'Madam, just give her six months. He is going to dump her. She will look hungry and lean, and then it is *you* he will come for.' It is the same Igbo women who scrambled into the bus that had been hired to take the townspeople to the village after the wedding.

'He doesn't love this woman, you should know that,' consoled my lawyer. 'It is purely a question of status. It is expected of him, and he is not in the wrong. Ask anyone and they will tell you.' After thirty-three years of marriage, I don't need sugar syrup to hide the bitterness of the pill. The voices from the subterranean depths within me have never failed me.

Fingers plunged into pounded yam and *egusi* soup. Everyone was amply fed and then the chief's wedding presents were displayed in the centre of the compound. Crates of mineral drinks, cartons of beer, several heads of fine tobacco, a mound of yam tubers, a goat, a trunk full of wrappers, shoes and underwear. The crowds gasped; Blessing cheered. Benson's generosity, unknown during the three decades of our married life, received a public airing.

Next, it was dancing-time. The newly married couple got up to dance as the drummers moved closer and the money 'spraying' began. Blessing dug the naira notes into the dust with the heels of her shiny black shoes as she danced. This was the part she enjoyed most. With youthful gaiety, she tilted her backside provocatively in my direction and danced. The head-tie tumbled into the dust and had to be picked up and rammed back on her head. As the chief, Benson carried himself sedately and danced with caution. The women fluttering about like giant moths in lace, brocade and gem-studded organza wrappers landed in the middle of the dancing arena. Unmindful of the elderly aunt with the jute bag, scrambling on all fours for the naira notes, between painted toenails, they danced. Every joint vibrated, every body part moved separately and in unison, according to the dictates of the rhythm. Arms akimbo they shook; their bosoms trembled. It was as if they were in a trance. The men applauded.

After a decent interval I got up to join my partners in marriage in this celebratory dance. The musicians struck up a new rhythm on seeing me, and the video cameras edged closer. But within minutes I was shoved this way and that by the money-sprayers and money-gatherers who were trying to get closer to the newly married couple, and I retired exasperated to my seat.

'Drat!' I fumed, lighting a cigarette, 'Did you see that?'

Benson, looking over his shoulder, caught my eye and seeing the expression on my face, beckoned to me to join him and Blessing once more. When I went up again, fag in hand, he put one arm over my shoulder, another on Blessing's and danced gleefully. His joy was complete.

'He planned this a long time ago,' I shouted above the noise to Jean. 'He is going to pay for it!'

Try as I did, it was impossible for me to imagine Benson, a British-trained engineer, and eighteen-year-old Blessing, barely out of school, sitting down and starting life together as man and wife. But then, maybe people don't sit down together to start anything anymore. They just get on with it. What makes us more qualified to be wives than the Blessings of the world? Love, Proposal, Acceptance, Registry Office Wedding, and a Piece of Paper, precisely in that order? Here was another set of rituals that made perfect sense to the people of this village and gave Blessing the legitimacy of a wife.

I announce to the expatriate club of like-minded women that I was leaving.

'I should have done this a long time ago,' moans Helen. 'I sit like a Wedgwood ornament on the top shelf, gathering dust . . . Things go on around me, but I am not consulted about anything.'

I tell them it's a new beginning. I talk about living for myself—I'll go to the cinema, I say, the theatre, there will be water in the taps, no electricity cuts, I toss in a Caribbean cruise for effect. It is hard to work up an enthusiasm for a life you haven't opted for but has been quite suddenly thrust upon you.

I grope for a lifeline. The younger women in the club see me as their hero, throwing it all in, and bravely venturing out into God knows where. The mercenary among them are shocked that I am leaving this country as I had entered the world—with a 'naked bottom' in Russian parlance. It's not so much the man's betrayal, but the fact that I allowed myself to be cheated out of a life, without pulling the rug from under his feet first. Benson, who does the laundry? Two sets of clothes pegs?

Never do anything without putting up a fight first, an old aunt in the village had advised me with deep intuition. The men appreciated fighting women who claimed their rightful place, as Wife Number One, Wife Number Two, Wife Dispossessed, whatever, who articulated their grievances in colourful, poetic abuse.

But at fifty-two, I am spent, while Benson has gotten himself a new lease of life. This is the age for the loosening of bonds and whittling down to the core . . . not a time to make new enemies as Voltaire said on his deathbed when asked if he would accept Christ and denounce the devil.

golden opportunities

The caption under the wedding photograph in the local newspaper read, 'Claude hooks Hope', as a matronly and obviously pregnant Hope, in white wedding dress and veil, stuffed a much-too-large piece of cake into the mouth of a bewildered and be-gloved Claude. Hope looked triumphant as the one who had 'hooked' Claude!

Our wedding picture was not quite so conventional. The photographer had me sitting on one of those wooden playground swings (a studio creation, of course), while my husband clutched at the chains. Very romantic, like a scene from the Indian movies. That was how I took my plunge into matrimony.

It has been not just a turn on the swing but a regular roller-coaster ride ever since. My friend Daphne says that the sharp bit goes out of a situation if you stick it out long enough, and that you arrive at a sort of benign indifference where the boat doesn't rock too badly, even if you keep wishing at the back of your mind that you were in a different boat.

My husband tends to be philosophical about these things. He maintains that women get the men they deserve and vice versa. I don't know if Kemi deserved the man she got, but she wasn't going to wait to find out.

When my husband told me his friend Debo's wife was coming from Lagos to stay the weekend with us, I felt the usual tingle of resentment. I disliked strange city-women even before I met them. Kemi was coming to see her son, who was at a boarding school in our town. It was his free weekend. Debo and my husband had been at school together, but it was twenty years later, with both engaged in different occupations, when their paths crossed again in Lagos. They were both following up payments for completed army contracts.

I had written Debo off from the start when I heard that he had two wives. Two wives and six children at forty! He must be one of those unreliable men, a womanizer, a spendthrift, a man who squandered his money on cars and clubs, I concluded. The two wives lived apart, in separate houses, with Debo doing the rounds between them. For all practical purposes, he lived with Kemi, his first wife. But it was Biola my husband talked about, Biola who was shy, Biola who was mild-mannered and soft-spoken, Biola who baked cakes. Biola was Debo's showpiece. Kemi was an unknown quantity, and I didn't look forward to entertaining this Lagos woman, an employee of the National Shipping Company, at my home.

I stayed longer at work than usual, knowing my husband was at the airport to meet Kemi. On her arrival, Kemi bounced her way up the stairs and took me completely by surprise. After the initial welcome and introductions, we settled ourselves in the living room. Kemi sat across from my husband, her miniskirt tight about her thighs. He stared at her legs all evening, from the ebony calves up the smooth shaven legs to where the patchwork leather skirt ended. Her puffy childlike hands had rings on every finger. The painted fingernails danced wildly as she gesticulated. She had an endless repertoire of stories, from corruption in high places to armed robbery and drug dealing. She spun them out with confidence, shaking the silky brown hairpiece that was unobtrusively attached to her hair by a silver clasp. She was thirty-eight but looked and acted about twenty-five.

She punctuated her conversation with 'Darling, you have no idea . . .!' She rolled her big brown eyes and said, 'I'm going to leave him. You wait and see. I'm just praying that God will give me a good man. That's it.' With the appropriate gestures, she washed her hands of Debo. I rushed around to make her bed and carried a bucket of hot water to her bathroom. She sat like a princess and, when everything was set, took herself to the bedroom on her spiky-heeled patent leather shoes.

Over the next two days, it was a total surprise every time Kemi emerged from the bedroom. You could never predict what the outfit might be. On Saturday morning, it was a burgundy wrapper and a flamboyant head-tie, with red lipstick that generously covered her lips. The pale edge of the wrapper read, 'Guaranteed Dutch Wax.' In the evening, it was striped culottes in black and white, the style accentuating her well-endowed bosom, and gold-studded sandals. On Sunday, it was a *boubou* in gold that trailed after her, sweeping the harmattan dust off my floor.

I didn't expect her to come into my kitchen, but there she was, blending the pepper and tomatoes, and browning the oxtail with Maggi cubes, early on Saturday morning. 'Darling, we have to be at the boarding school by ten o'clock,' she said, pouring a gallon of oil into the stew. So we cooked and we talked.

As she diced the carrots for the *jollof* rice, I noticed her smooth, well-rounded wrists and the pearl-studded gold bangle that fitted tightly around her wrist. 'Can we buy Kemi a gift? It's her first visit with us,' my husband had inquired, opening his wallet. 'Buy her something personal, like a bangle,' he had added. I had thought of something neutral, like an enamel saucepan or a Melaware tray.

'It's good to be independent,' Kemi said, 'then you can tell these men to go to hell!'

'How do you cope with your . . . with Biola, I mean?' I hesitated.

'Darling, I'm Debo's only wife!' she responded. 'If he chooses to keep a prostitute somewhere, that's his problem.' She volunteered more information, letting me in on a secret.

'Biola used medicine. She goes to a *mallam*, and that's how she trapped Debo. I can't forgive Debo. I have had two children and four miscarriages. Every time I miscarried, Biola got pregnant. It's the medicine.'

I warmed up to Kemi. 'Taste the stew,' she said, offering me a spoonful. The pepper singed my tongue and set my intestines aflame. 'It's too cold in this town,' she reasoned, 'You have to eat plenty of pepper.'

Her job with the National Shipping Company kept her comfortable, and her contracts in Lagos gave her access to all sorts of loans. She was building a block of apartments. And she was into the supply business, buying *garri* in bulk from the factory in Ibadan and supplying colleagues and friends every two weeks. She had her social clubs: the Inner Wheel, the Esteem Sisters, Oshodi Women's Club, and the Fellowship of Business Women International. They met in each other's homes, drank beer and other local brew, and consumed huge quantities of fried meat and fish.

'You should come to Lagos,' she invited me, squeezing my hand. 'I have grand things planned for you.'

Biola was the bane of her existence. 'Do you know Biola has two children by an Alhaji, and she's now pregnant by an Igbo man?'

'What does Debo see in her?' I prompted.

'Darling, she is ugly—crooked front teeth, skinny, in *buba* and wrapper. Oily, pimply face—that's the type Debo goes for . . . I'm just waiting for a nice man to come my way,' she concluded.

We got in the car. As we drove past the market, Kemi beckoned to me to stop at one of the shops. It was pretty much a shack, with wooden boards hastily nailed together, the nails still sticking out. 'Come to Blessed Spot and Enjoy Yourself,' urged a piece of paper nailed to the board. In this haven of bliss, this oasis, there stood a Coke machine in one corner and a photocopying machine in another. A cupboard with a glass front, roughly put together, housed lotions, creams, and other cosmetics in jars with orange, pink and purple tops.

'How much is that facial mask?' Kemi asked the girl, who was squeezed between the various gadgets.

'Forty naira.'

'What about the nail hardener?'

'Thirty-five naira.'

I shifted and discreetly eyed Kemi. What was she going to ask for next? After much haggling, Kemi declared that these things were cheaper in Lagos anyway, and promptly left.

We brought her eleven-year-old son, a scrawny lad with unkempt hair, dry scaly skin, and a shell-shocked look, home from the boarding school to spend Saturday with us. Kemi gave a crisp twenty-naira note to the master in charge of the dormitory for his newborn child. 'Boy or girl?' she inquired, intending to send a gift on her return to Lagos. The chief prefect and the hall messenger got twenty naira each, to 'keep an eye' on the eleven-year-old Dele. 'He has to pass his exams. I'll hold you responsible,' she teased the chief prefect as she tucked the twenty-naira note into his palm. Once home, Dele was scrubbed from head to toe, washed, bleached, and disinfected, and fed a generous helping of *jollof* rice and the pepper stew loaded with oxtail, liver, and other choice cuts of meat. There was a brisk and practical air about it all—she had come from Lagos to do a job, and she had to do it well. Dele's appearance, lectures on studying hard, compliance with authority, taking care of personal belongings—she seemed to tick things off one by one on her mental agenda. Later in the day, we took Dele back to suffer the rigours of boarding-school life.

Kemi and I sat down to a cup of coffee. 'My life has been wasted on Debo,' she moaned, 'when I think about it, I get palpitations.' She talked of injustice, and it seemed as if all men were ogres exploiting and deceiving their wives, and lavishing love and money on mistresses. We exchanged stories of betrayal, of husbands who drove us to the outer limits of despair. It was our inner strength that had saved us from high blood pressure and heart attacks. We had acquired wisdom through experience.

Kemi couldn't sustain this sombre mood for long. As I brought the second cup of coffee, she launched into stories of erring husbands who got involved with several women and then dropped dead, leaving a labyrinth of woes for their wives. Lorraine, her friend, stood in her black scarf and black wrapper, she said, the picture of wifely grief, flanked by the boys on one side and the girls on the other. Kehinde, the 'other woman', had burst in on them at the funeral, also clad in black, holding two children by the hand and a baby

44

on her back. Lorraine was hysterical, Kemi said. 'You won't have peace where you are going,' she screamed to the man in the box, rigid in embalmed serenity. 'It's not the kingdom of God you are heading for. You'd better get up and sort out this mess!' I laughed till my sides hurt.

'How much do you have in the bank?' Kemi inquired casually. 'You know, I could send you wrappers and shoes from Lagos. Just add your profit and sell them quietly. Before you know it, you can buy a piece of land and put a few bricks on it. Then, like Debo, your husband will come to you when he needs a mere five hundred naira.'

I had meagre savings, put together erratically over a period of ten years. In a household such as ours, it wasn't easy to operate a bank account without my husband finding out about it. I hid the savings book and switched its place periodically—and panicked about being found out. My husband and I operated a joint account that was perpetually in the red.

My husband was not a notoriously difficult man, but Kemi's presence made the differences in our outlook more pronounced. He was the kind that filled his tank every time he passed the petrol station, while I flogged the old Toyota on reserve and then grudgingly drove in for maybe a quarter-tank of gas. He coaxed his car, keeping it in top form, changing its tyres periodically, checking its brakes. I left the windows down in the rain; I cursed the old car when it jerked and threatened to give up on me. All the trash over the past six months accumulated on the floor of my car—drugstore receipts, church programmes, candy wrappers, and you would even find an odd potato or onion nestling under the seat. The children treated my car with scant respect. My husband's car radio played blues and jazz while he cruised along. He talked about joining the Road Safety Campaign.

I mulled over Kemi's proposal through the night. Lying in bed, I looked around the room. There were landmarks everywhere, milestones, souvenirs of my quarrels with my husband over other women, real and imagined, and my attempts to get even with him. The Sony cassette-player marked a major quarrel, when I rushed out and bought it as something belonging to me. I was going to put my feet up and listen to music. Another heated argument resulted in expensive lace curtains. The shrouded figures emerged one by one from the closet, women who inhabited my bedroom in silhouetted shapes, lurking in corners, insinuating themselves between the sheets. The names spilt out, echoing around my bed. I had never had an instinct for business or the initiative, but Kemi was going to launch me into the world of *garri* and palm-oil entrepreneurs. My life was at a crossroads, and the horizon held innumerable pots of gold.

Kemi and I entered the bank. 'Do not abuse the naira. Handle it with care,' said the Central Bank poster, with pictures of grubby and bacteria-ridden currency notes changing hands, tucked into sweaty blouses, in traders' pouches attached to petticoats, and crumpled into unrecognizable shapes by newspaper vendors. The shiny coins were so much better, though coins made you feel poorer than you were and made your purse heavier. I stretched out my hand to present the withdrawal slip to the cashier. A whiff of sardine-odour emanated from the lady standing next to me; she continued with her crocheting, oblivious to everything around her.

Kemi and I sat down on the bench. The women looked colourful, the men drab. Tight clothes reduced the sperm count, Kemi said. Sitting back, I watched backsides, big and small, in trousers, skirts, and wrappers, all provocatively tight. A woman with a baby sat near us. The baby bounced about and played with her fingers. Then, without warning, it pissed all over the man sitting next to the mother.

'Baby don piss O!' cried the man, jumping from his seat.

'Sorry O,' said the mother, mopping up with a piece of tissue from her handbag.

The baby said, 'Come, come.'

'No way,' said the man good-humouredly, gathering his naira notes and hurrying out of the bank. I handled my savings—with trepidation—as Kemi and I walked out of the bank. I felt hollow inside, having emptied out my savings account. I quickly put the money in an envelope and gave it to Kemi.

'Darling, just give me one week—seven days—and I'll be in touch.'

It is almost two years since Kemi's visit. I wait for letters and parcels and the passport to entrepreneurship and that peculiar independence that only Kemi could envisage. Maybe she has completed her block of flats at Oshodi and moved in; maybe her prayers have been answered and God has given her that 'nice man'.

She had left behind a souvenir though—her gold-studded slippers, and lipstick on the edges of my coffee mug.

jaded appetites

She walked in with this man, her lover. A married man with three children, I was told later. She fussed over him like a wife does (or is it mistresses that fuss?). She made him orange juice first, freshly squeezed, and then tea, hovered over him, and made recordings of Chopin and Brahms for him, lolling on my carpets. He liked classical music. Could she be in love this time, I wondered, with a man who looked anchored and tethered in a starched white shirt and tie, unavailable? It was written all over his face. Greeting him was clumsy—not the usual How's the wife? How're the children? How's work? but . . . How's life?

Perhaps she was a timely distraction. What was in it for her? She seemed to have her eyes wide open and feet planted firmly on the ground. Perhaps he had stumbled in her path at a time when she needed a man in her life. When it came to goodbyes she wouldn't look back. There would be no messy emotions, no awkward entanglements, no strings or covenants.

He called her every morning on getting to the office. She made his day, he said, with as much originality as possible. She on her part did not interfere with his family life. He dropped the children off at school, paid the electricity bill and cashed a cheque for his wife at the bank before getting to the office.

After work, he drove to her love nest and she sent him home dutifully to his wife when the clock struck ten and when all respectable men should be home. They knew the terms. He was decent, a family man, and a father.

Why should I entertain this adulterous pair in my home? I protested to myself initially. She was a link in the convoluted extended family chain, with an audacious claim to my space, but he was not. But they were a compelling distraction and I found myself acting the spellbound audience to their superbly orchestrated drama. Will he? Won't he? Will she? Why he? She was so utterly relaxed in his company, this travelling companion, this proverbial part-time lover. She went out of the way to fill in the gaps left by his wife. The dresses short enough to provoke desire but just long enough to ward off unwanted attention. The special perfume, which he alone would recognize and sniff her out in a crowd. She picked a rose from the vase on my dining table and gave it to him. I began to enjoy their company in a curious sort of way like being in the midst of a West Indian carnival, the steel band urging you to dance. They were so nice to each other. It seemed like good times all the way.

They were leaving that afternoon. She brought out the food flask and went about packing lunch for her lover. He had a touch of ulcer in the stomach, she said, and wasn't to go for long periods without a snack. She meticulously arranged the ricé and stew and vegetables in the food flask. There was water in the cooler and orange juice in a separate bottle.

I looked on amused. So this is what every mistress aspires to be! A wife! To have a man to pamper and take care of, with an I-know-you-better-than-your-wife-does claim to his person. And the magazines are never tired of telling us we should be as tantalizing and mysterious as mistresses!

'It's not that I want him to be with me all the time,' she confided. 'It's just that I wish I knew where he goes every weekend.' I searched my mind for expert advice.

'Be prepared to put in ninety-five per cent,' I said with wifely wizardry, 'and expect five per cent in return. Did your mother know where your father went each day? Did she needle him about his day-to-day activities?'

She came in with a flourish the next time, like a newly wedded wife, he, close behind her like the bridegroom who had just acquired a spouse. I was mildly surprised that they were still together and that her pace of living had room for Part Two of the love episode.

No sooner had she come in, she started preparing his late-night snack (he had ulcer, remember?). With an artistic hand she trimmed the edges of the bread, put slices of cheese and a fried egg in between and stacked the sandwiches. The flask had hot water for his cocoa.

'What's for breakfast?' she enquired jokingly as she climbed in the car beside him for their rendezvous at the Night Club.

'I'll have to ask the chef,' I replied laughing.

During each visit she spent long hours in the kitchen catering to her lover's tastes. 'Hey, that's what a wife's supposed to be doing,' I taunted her. She was in a black shift with gold buttons. She launched on a tirade over his wife on that occasion.

'Wife! I'm not trying to run her down because she is his wife. But the woman is downright lazy! What does she do with her money? He takes care of everything in the home. If he doesn't buy soap, there's no soap in the house. She doesn't even bother about her looks. I have never met her, but they say she is very shabby. If the car breaks down on her way to work, she leaves it on the road and goes to look for him, instead of getting a mechanic. What kind of woman is that? And you know him . . . He is a person who does not open his mouth to talk. He just allows things to be as they are.'

The orange juice, the sandwiches, the crayfish stews got richer to make up amply for what he was missing in his wife. He seemed to be carrying a cross—wife, children and extended family. She needed to be there to make his life bearable.

It was an afternoon in March when she arrived with her lover. He wore a blue-checked sports shirt unbuttoned sufficiently to reveal the gold chain and the hairy chest. He read newspapers in the living room and watched video films. She busied herself turning my kitchen upside down on his account. It was a pleasant confusion when she was around. She rummaged around frying eggs, cooking spaghetti—everything had to be in style, extravagant and in abundance.

When all was done, she opened my cupboards, brought out the best crockery and cutlery and served the man. Her quaintly self-mocking domestic routine amused the household. They could never be man and wife, I consoled myself, doing things for each other every day, bearing the hurts, rejections, misunderstandings and still sitting down to a meal together over red roses.

They could, however, carry out their connubial act at periodic intervals in someone else's home. That was all the husband she needed and that was all the petting he could take from her. When they drove out of the town, they went their separate ways, he to his family, and she to the empty concrete bungalow in the government residential area, with damaged fly-screens on the veranda and ceiling stained by rain-water.

He kept up the semblance of untiring love, it seemed to me, in a relationship that had 'missed the road'. 'Anything might happen' was the closest he came to reassurance when she looked at him with suspicion. She broached the subject of having a child (doesn't every woman want to be a mother?). 'Your life has been peaceful,' he said cleverly, piling tenderness on concern, 'I wouldn't want to inflict a child on you.' He got out of it that time. She sensed the meaning and ordered him out. He came back the following week. 'Who wants a child, anyway?' she said, slipping into the patent leather shoes and swinging her hips out of the door. That was what he wanted to hear. He wished to leave no trace, no fingerprints, no sign of his having been with her. No endearments in public, he had cautioned her at the start of their relationship—'I am a family man.' She accepted his conditions though it irked her that the plastic rose in cellophane which she had sent him had to be hidden in the bottom drawer of his desk at work, and the card with the cushioned and quilted heart, stuffed amidst memos in his briefcase. They had, however, celebrated the first anniversary of their friendship with gifts and a meal at a Chinese restaurant. She had positioned herself, with time, as the band-aid, the balm to massage his withering ego and sustain him through midlife crises.

At breakfast, she was in the kitchen with a bottle of Coke and a chunk of bread, contemplating her next move. The conversation kept going back to Armstrong's irresponsible wife who scrimped on soap and toilet paper, and sent the children to bed with *garri* and water. So what was new?

It was our tenth wedding anniversary. I tried the crayfish stew and spaghetti laced with corned beef on my husband. My gold-fringed card on the table was gushing with sentiment. His was spare. Love for him was a benign presence like allowing the dog to lie in the kitchen and not kicking it.

❖

It was June. The rain blotted out the maize farms, the corrugated zinc roofs and the blue hills beyond. She and her lover came in under one umbrella, their cheerful prattle reaching me long before their entwined bodies entered the kitchen. Armstrong was bare-chested as usual, I noticed through a malarial haze. He was most deferential like he was responsible for my fever. I felt an intense irritation that he was a fake, phoney, a conman, a hyena in club-gear.

She was buoyant and porous, without a care in the world, a gaily coloured gypsy shawl thrown over her pink linen blouse with careless abandon. Her hair was done in a thousand braids, a style that must have taken at least eight hours of patient sitting. I was only half aware of what was going on as they both took over the house. Chickens were hacked out of the freezer, the aroma of smoked sardine and ginger, which may have seemed inviting when I was well, nauseated me. It was Armstrong's tastes and needs and his ulcerous appetite that were being satiated to the full.

The lover, in the meantime, read *Time* and *Newsweek* in the lounge, and looked up occasionally at Schwarzenegger's stunts on video. He had domesticated himself into a cosy brother-in-law or someone equally respectable in the eyes of the household. He threw one leg over the arm of my upholstered chair and discussed politics. The children had stopped their whispering and tittering in corridors and had accepted him as Uncle Armstrong. From time to time she ordered them into the kitchen to hand-squeeze a batch of oranges for Armstrong, for his midday juice, or to assist in some chore that was to make life more comfortable for him.

'So when is the big day?' I teased, holding the throbbing sides of my head.

'What big day?' she asked, 'Me? . . . I can never be a wife. You know that!'

'What do you think you are now? As slavish and mulish as a wife! All these three-course meals, sandwiches and ulcer remedies!'.

'It's only because it's temporary. In two days' time his wife will be sweating over the kitchen stove while I will be free. Going about my business. No man breathing down my neck.'

'You sound as if you don't enjoy it.'

'I enjoy my freedom . . . I admire you wives,' she patronized, 'for your faithfulness. But it will drive me crazy.'

The house assumed prison-like proportions as my fever raged. When I was a child, illness left me shrinking like a punctured balloon while my pillow grew bigger and bigger. Now, my head was like a giant slab of lead, my stomach squeamish. I had no inclination for food or books or sporting lovers under my roof. The heavy damask curtains shut out air, light and human warmth. There was an eerie silence in my room while the rest of the world hummed with activity. What about spare ribs tonight, she asked, sticking her head through a crack in the door. It meant Armstrong felt like spare ribs, how about having some tonight? I had looked at the two of them through rose-coloured spectacles, a romantic pair in an unreal world, like the monarch butterflies of Mexico, excellent fodder for a short story. But it was becoming an expensive story with no dramatic turns or climaxes. I began to tire of

Armstrong the lover—beneath those sporty clothes was a devious lout, I concluded. I began to feel sorry for his wife, the rejected woman, perhaps an attractive lawyer or teacher, on a couch in the husbandless living room with a faraway look in her eyes. Three little children in front of the television set. Maybe.

The visit that followed was somewhat subdued. He watched Wimbledon tennis on TV. He promised to buy her an iPad on that trip, she said. He was hurt that she didn't ever ask him for anything. 'How do I know you love me if you don't depend on me!' he said. She wore a green silk dress and an embroidered Indian jacket over it. Her hair was permed. He looked wispy and frail beside her, pale and asthmatic. She ate continually from the moment she stepped in the door, a mango first, followed by some chocolates she found in the fridge, and then rice and pepper-stew. He will tire of her if she doesn't watch her weight, I thought to myself. There was a restlessness about her, she seemed constantly to be several jumps ahead.

They breezed in at the start of the harmattan, when the yellow flowers covered the hillside, a last burst of blossom before the prolonged dry season. She looked a bit blasé about life in general but still hadn't lost the ardour to cook for her lover. She started with great enthusiasm, which wore off after the elaborate palm-nut kernel stew had been prepared. There had been grand plans for goat-head pepper soup (for Armstrong's supper) but all she seemed capable of doing was throwing an egg in hot oil and slamming it on a slice of bread.

She repeated that wives were tied hand and foot to their husbands but she was free as the wind. She could take off when she wanted to, and come back as she pleased. She wore a cool, summer outfit, a Middle-Eastern kaftan in a swirl of pastel colours. It was a gift from Armstrong, she said, something special he had purchased on his travels, wrapped in tinsel and sent to her office as a surprise. We went shopping. She tried to fit Armstrong into every fancy shirt she saw hanging at the shop window. And then, as we drove around the traffic island with the gasping, concrete fish in the middle, we saw it. There, below the Coca-Cola advertisement, on the pavement hung a dozen kaftans in identical styles and a riot of colours!

It was three days to Christmas. I had baskets of tomatoes sitting around the kitchen, waiting to be puréed. I was cleaning and cutting a chicken at the sink when they walked in. Armstrong retired to the study to look for foreign newspapers while she started the cooking, laboriously, climbing over my tomatoes and cluttering up my sideboards. He likes his food cooked in special ways. No, they couldn't join us for lunch. The black-eyed beans had to have a touch of crayfish, and a couple of Maggi cubes thrown in. The onions and tomatoes had to be blended and fried, not chopped up. 'I pity his wife,' I provoked, 'if he is that choosy about his meals.'

The next morning, over *akamu* and *kosai*, she startled me by saying that she was preparing herself to be free of Armstrong the veterinary surgeon. He was too much of a family man, that was his problem. Christmas, Easter, Ramadan, Independence Day—he insisted on spending time with his family. After all . . . his wife . . . and she stopped. What of his wife, I asked, perking up. Was she still as loose as ever? Her eyes brightened. 'What do you say to a man who caught his wife with someone else—red-handed—yet won't ask her any questions?'

I could see that she had run out of stories. Old stories kept resurfacing with fresh details and new emotions. She had a pageboy hairstyle with a bang that she kept sweeping back. Black satin blouse over mini skirt, with a walkman attached to her hips and headphones plugged to her ears. 'Is this new?' I signalled.

'My new boyfriend—he gave it to me,' she mouthed, tapping her toes to the music being piped into her ears. The new man was a pharmacist. The indigestion since the previous visit had brought about a meeting. He was crazy about her, she said. Armstrong sat reading the newspapers. When the meal was ready, she served him an enormous mound of pounded yam and spinach stew, and followed it up with a single orange on a plastic plate, seductively cleft. She sat herself across from him like a fond wife and smiled mysteriously.

On the way to the car, she picked a rose—'For my love,' she said.

'Which one?' I asked.

The New Year saw her in leg warmers and polyester skirt. She made her way to the kitchen tucking in a sausage roll she picked up on the way. I was having my kitchen units painted. The painters were everywhere, climbing up, crawling under—she seemed to be quite unmindful of their presence. She started dicing, chopping, shredding and frying as she rested a massive elbow and thigh against my newly painted kitchen units. The black polyester skirt acquired a huge smudge of white where her thigh peeped through the slit in the skirt.

'O my God!' she screamed, turning to the painter. 'I'll sue you for this. You've ruined my skirt.' Then she stuck her leg out to him and indicated that he clean the paint with whatever was at his disposal. The painter first tried the skirt, then let his hand run over her thigh as he rubbed the paint off gently.

Armstrong had in the meantime stretched himself on the couch in the living room.

Her theory now was that you should get rid of a man before he asked you to quit. So she was on the path towards easing Armstrong, her man on the moon, out of her life. It was only a matter of time. She had given up hoping that his wife would drop dead or that he would acquire the guts to abandon her. She talked about Yinka the pharmacist who played polo and drank pure mineral water in the club. She served Armstrong his spaghetti garnished with fried plantain and turned around and continued her story of Yinka—'He's a wa-a-arm person,' she said. Of course, he wasn't totally unattached. There was this fiancée of his who was childish and temperamental and he was growing tired of her anyway.

'The places she visits,' she said with a meaningful look. 'I wouldn't be seen dead in them.' She had developed a taste for jazz as that was Yinka's favourite kind of music.

She curled up like a large pussycat, head resting on Armstrong's lap and watched junk movies for the rest of the day. I made Armstrong a cheese sandwich and packed his supper in the food flasks.

legacies

Deep in that yam country in the middle of paradise itself, where the landscape opens out in different shades of green, lies Adoka village and the Ode Ogbole compound. There are miles and miles of yam mounds, as far as the eye can see, and orange groves, with a compound situated in the corner of each plot of land, some more prosperous than the others.

Here, when a ninety-year-old man dies, it is not a departure. It is indeed a transition to the great beyond. You can't help thinking that he lives on in those acres of yam country, in those gigantic trees, in those muscular sons, strapping daughters and grandchildren who have come after him. His legacy lives on and is everywhere. He has become a presiding spirit infused in the lives of his descendants.

The dirt road stretches out interminably from the turn-off on the highway to the east of the country. There are schools and compounds and Pentecostal churches at every bend. The early missionaries appeared to have made their entry here with education first, and then with the Bible. The culture embraced Christianity and made it its own, the hymns were set to the solemn beat of Idoma music. A single drum throbbed as a large church choir, about 100 members sat on wooden benches and sang. It was continuous, it flowed like a river, it had no beginning or end, just a continual swaying, hypnotic and solemn. The listeners swayed with it. The women cooking over wood fires swayed with it. The sons bustling about making arrangements for the funeral swayed with it. The children romping in the dust swayed. It caught everyone in its enthralling grip, sinuous, fluid, and melodious. The father of the clan was being serenaded like a prince to the other world.

It was a time for reunions. Sister Ify's brother whom we had never met before had come from Kano; Sister Eunice from Lagos, Sister Phoebe from a distant town in the north-east whose name nobody knew how to pronounce. Greetings and introductions and laughter rang out. Each son entertained his 'in-laws' and guests in his own house in the compound. The heat made it impossible for anyone to remain indoors for long, so most of the entertainment took place outside. There was a canopy erected outside Aaron's house for his own guests, and plastic chairs stacked in its shade. While the men sat there and rested from their travel with local brew, the women got busy on one side of the house where the outdoor cooking had begun. The conversation was muted and animated in turns.

Chopping the okra on a wooden board balanced on her knee, Sister Eunice 'gisted' about life in Lagos, an exhausting round of parties she said. Today this friend is having pink *ashebi* as the uniform for her birthday party, tomorrow it is grey and silver *aso oke* for a friend's wedding anniversary; the day after it is red damask head-tie for a niece's wedding.

You keep buying clothes and accessories on credit so as not to be left out, and your debt increases. This is life in Lagos, she said. Sister Beatrice from Port Harcourt was in charge of the *egusi* soup. She washed the giant slabs of stock fish tenderly, shredded the dark green *ugwu* leaves with great expertise and got even the Maggi cubes removed from their wrappers ready to start the soup. You swear by the *ugwu* leaf in Igboland, she said. It had all sorts of medicinal properties, such that you could soak and squeeze the leaves, drink the liquid and come out fortified, and less anaemic. Two hefty women pounded the yam in a huge mortar as steam rose from it and sweat dripped off their arms and necks. More yams were brought out of the store for boiling as cars pulled up in the distance and more city guests arrived. Each yam belonged to a particular variety, it was the connoisseur who knew which was intended for pounding, which for frying, for boiling, etc., and which combination gave the right consistency of pounded yam. There was art and skill, and Sister Ify supervised. Titi served those who came with their plates and made sure no one dipped their fingers into the soup-pot, unsolicited.

I busied myself, impressed by the order and discipline which emerges on these occasions without anyone imposing it over the situation. The men were fed first.

'Do you know something,' sister Eunice continued, 'Idoma men have a curious way of complimenting their wives on their cooking? When they relish the meal that has been placed before them, they say to the wife, where is "that thing" you served a moment ago? When there is no talk, you know that the meal had nothing to recommend it.'

Women ate as they cooked. Brother Daniel's 'in-laws' had come from the neighbouring villages 'to lend support'. They sat in a row on the veranda of his home, facing each other with a steaming mound of pounded yam in front, and a common bowl of soup. Into it they dipped their fingers in turn and ate till each was satisfied. A generator set hummed in the distance and kept basic lighting on for the entire Ode Ogbole compound. We had a cold-water shower, taking turns in the bathroom, and retired for the night.

The drumming and the singing went on all through the night as I swayed myself to sleep. Our guests slept on mats in the living room. The day began early but time moved slowly. The women were all at their posts again making bean-fry and millet porridge for breakfast. They ate huge bowls full of the porridge accompanied by the bean-fry and whatever else was available. The chairs were being arranged for the funeral. More canopies came in. A water tanker was parked in front of the compound.

The women from the various houses fetched water in enamel basins. Ada was the chief water-carrier. Tirelessly, she carried water on her head and filled the various water-drums in the house.

Towards 9 o'clock people had their baths one by one and got ready in their *aso oke*, lace and damask. This was not to be a mourning but a celebration of Papa Ogbole's life.

'Brother Inusa's getting old O! He wants hot water for a bath!' said Sister Ify laughing, putting finishing touches to the bougainvillea wreath being assembled.

Aunty Becky sat on the bed while Sister Eunice started winding and knotting a piece of damask around her head. 'Do it Miriam Babangida style—a bit tighter,' she said as she peered into a hand-held mirror.

The local guests started arriving and took their places under the canopies. Each canopy was for a particular group of people—the church had its canopy with all the clergy fitted out in their collars; the visitors from Abuja (government dignitaries) had their canopy; in-laws and villagers had their canopy each.

The Idoma service was brief, neat, without fanfare, and solemn. Papa's biography was read. It was a history not only of a hard-working and God-fearing individual but a history of the clan, the early church, and the arrival of the missionaries; a near-century of accomplishments, which included insurmountable barriers that had been breached to arrive at Papa's destination. The man who bridged two worlds, colonial and post-colonial, had crossed the great divide and joined his ancestors. Papa's descendants were introduced family by family, and asked to step out to the centre of the arena.

Brother Daniel's younger wife had waited for this moment. She and her husband were in white—her white lace was the type with lots of peep holes over one half and gem stones embedded over the rest. Perched on sleek, white high-heeled shoes, she walked to the middle stylishly and stood beside her husband. You'd think she had won the Miss Universe contest. She was quite stunning. Her children wore jeans and T-shirts and stood apart from the village children with their dusty feet and ill-fitting clothes. The senior wife also answered the call but was somehow eclipsed by the presence of the city wife. Sister Maria had appeared from somewhere; she had left the village in a huff years ago when her husband had abandoned her and gone off to Lagos to try his luck in the oil industry. She came back plump and fair, well bleached and prosperous. City life had indeed been good for her. Her husband who had also come in for the funeral stood apart, entirely unconnected from her.

Papa's wife was called out at the very end. In his eighties, as a widower of ten years, Papa's sons had married him a wife—a homely woman to keep his hearth warm, cook his meals, and be there to answer his needs. Mamma Ogbole was fifty-five years old. She had assumed the role of mother, and now the mantle of widowhood had fallen upon her.

The palm oil sizzled in the aluminium saucepan. Put in the stockfish, Sister Beatrice said. The choir sang 'Trust and Obey' in Idoma to a very unusual beat. We fanned ourselves with the funeral programme. Now add the onion and pepper and crayfish, Beatrice instructed. I threw in a dash of *dawa dawa* and a couple of Maggi cubes. The pall-bearers carried the coffin slowly to the grave site.

There was a stillness in the air, and the leaves on the trees stopped moving. Sister Eunice who had lost two children to malaria was no newcomer to death. She watched without blinking as bitter memories flooded her mind. The bougainvillea wreath was carried by the grandchildren to the grave site. The soup was bubbling furiously. Now add the ogbonno and keep stirring, said Beatrice. The *ugwu* leaves went in last so that they retained their colour and flavour.

The guests were seated now as Ada and Phoebe carried trays of rice and pounded yam and delivered them to the various tables. Someone stuck his head into the kitchen and said 'The pastors need mineral water—is there any pure water?'

'The chicken is for the visitors from Abuja,' Sister Ify reminded them as the girls hurried out with the trays.

Mineral drinks were opened and cartons of imported fruit juice.

'Sister Maria is crying—someone please go in and talk to her,' said Ify, as she rushed out to attend to the guests.

In the dark shadows of the bedroom, among piles of clothing, Maria sat on the edge of the bed weeping. The reality of her father's departure was just beginning to dawn on her. Mamma had been gone for some years now. Desolate and orphaned, the youngest of twelve children, she wept for Papa. When her husband left her it was Papa who had taken care of her children and her own needs as she wandered about looking for a place to settle. Papa had been an invisible strength and presence.

The masquerades arrived to distract the mourners. With the rustling of their straw skirts, whip in hand, they wove in and out of the crowds. The drumming continued as children ran after them provoking them to turn around and whip them. From time to time they would stop in front of the Abuja visitors and beg for money.

I watched one of the 'in-laws' from afar as he sat on a stool, bent down to the pounded yam, took each ball and moulded it at leisure between his fingers and palm, then holding it adroitly dipped it in the soup and swallowed it. The fingers went back to the bowl of pounded yam. It was a tableau, like the swaying of the Idoma choir, like the rhythmic pounding of the yam in wooden mortars enveloped in steam. Sister Ify brought out the souvenirs, calendars for everyone, special plastic trays for the Abuja guests, and plastic cups for the 'in-laws'. Papa in his early years smiled from the cups and trays and calendars. The four neighbouring villages had been given a cow each and several cartons of beer. This was a funeral they would talk about in years to come.

survivor

I don't know how she insinuated herself into our lives. I barely knew her. But she sent these little notes through her son to my office. She didn't even pronounce my name right and I didn't bother to correct her. She had the habit of showing up at my office with a head of lettuce in a plastic bag—'Got it real cheap, girl, from the farm,' she would say and dump it on my desk. Another time it was a visit to the bakery. She was going to introduce me to the best bargain in town. Melody Bread it was called. You half expected the loaf to start whistling as you sliced it. It was cheaper to buy bread straight off the baker's clay oven before it hit the supermarket shelves. Did I like pork, she enquired. She knew a place where pigs were slaughtered on Saturday mornings. Pork was cheaper than beef anyway. With pork fat you could save on margarine. She bought baskets of tomatoes in season and dumped them in the freezer. She advised me on re-fashioning old clothes rather than buying new ones, and introduced me to Yusuf, the Liberian tailor, who turned out these good-as-new culottes and tank tops for her.

We were sisters in spirit—in situation rather—in a country of beginnings. You were forever beginning, never forging ahead, always 'managing', just catching up. And when you thought you had got to the point where you could perhaps start a poultry farm in the backyard, armed robbers raided your house, stole your 1970 Peugeot 504, the Labour Congress called for a nationwide strike, and you started all over again. Democracy was set in motion, then the army stepped in and you were back where you began. For some it was a lifetime of beginnings. Others like Brenda stumbled ahead in an oblique bid to make a living in spite of numerous setbacks.

'Did you notice how Nigerian men never call their wives by name?' she asked me as we drove in her little blue Beetle, heading for one of her cost-saving ventures. 'As if they were goats or furniture or something.' But her husband called her Brin, she said, and she called him by his first name, which continually shocked her sisters-in-law.

I ran into her next when she was on the street arguing, holding a man by his collar, getting hysterical over something, her face and hair wet in the rain. Her aggressive driving combined with a sudden downpour had caused a man in his car to go off the road and land in a ditch. The man had emerged from the ditch in a fury, come up to her car and snatched her keys. That had unleashed Brenda's foul temper. She hit out at the man, screaming 'Gimme back my keys,' and when the man had cooled down sufficiently to return her keys she slapped him across the cheek before jerkily driving off. A gathering crowd of spectators looked aghast.

Brenda talked about the Dominican Republic like it was a piece of paradise itself—mostly in terms of food, lobsters, crabs, shrimps, everything that was in abundance there and totally unaffordable in our given circumstances. Is it not on the other side of Haiti, I asked, conjuring up visions of hungry children waiting on the shores to be spirited away to more prosperous lands. Maybe Brenda met Emeka in a palm-fringed ambience. Their wedding picture had the two of them in their finery, captured in a glowing wine glass—a photographic trick. If only they had remained in that ecstatic and inebriated state forever.

Every once in a while Emeka would roll up his metal garage door (a novel and noisy installation) and pull out his gleaming yellow Mercedes Benz. The car would stand outside his house for a couple of hours, decorating the yard with the chickens scratching amidst the corn, and the okra leaning over the driveway. Then he would climb in regally, in an *agbada* to match, and cruise out slowly down the bumpy dirt road. The children were allowed in the car only at Christmas time when, with his wife by his side in her enormous starched head-tie, children propped up rigidly, with clean hands and noses wiped, he took them to his hometown. It was a seven-hour drive during which he stopped for petrol and wandered into the bush a couple of times. But the children were not allowed to eat in the car or drink. So they arrived stiff and famished and dead beat in their Sunday best. His bank balance was known only to himself and to God. He made sure his wife knew nothing about what went in and came out. 'Is it not your women who are capable of poisoning their husbands for money?' Brenda taunted him.

Her favourite story was of the time Emeka gave her 500 naira to prepare the Stew of the Week. With that, Brenda went to the market, bought the ingredients, cooked the meal lovingly and served it at the table before inviting her husband to eat. One day the table was set elaborately as usual, with his placemat, his plate with a porcelain lid covering the food, the water poured into his glass, flowers in the vase. With a keen appetite he sat down, washed his hands and lifted the porcelain lid. There, on his plate in the centre, sat his 500-naira note. No food. 'How do you expect me to cook with the money you gave me?' asked Brenda, coming in from the kitchen, toothpick in hand. I knew then that the outsider had acquired the tricks of the insider.

She had the air of someone constantly improving herself, whether it was in the food she cooked, the plants she tended to or in her relationship with her husband. She read books like *The Perfect Woman* and *The Misunderstood Man*, and gave out advice freely, garnered from pulp fiction. She read out portions from the *Family Circle Magazine* as we waited in a petrol queue, our cars parked bumper to bumper.

'Be your partner's best friend. Show a real interest in his life. Celebrate his successes and empathize with his hurts and frustrations,' she read. 'And girl, this is for you,' she continued. 'Be a partner not a parent. Care for him but don't hover.'

'I don't hover,' I said.

'You smother,' she said, flipping the pages to recipes.

'And how about you and Emeka . . .?'

'We're all right as far as he's concerned. As long as I don't do or say the wrong thing. And don't rock the boat by wanting something he doesn't.'

I could tell that she was through with perfuming the sheets and lingering at the doorway till his car disappeared from view.

✤

Brenda surfaced after three months and breezed into our living room as if she had never left it. She was chirpy, excitable, curious and facetious, all at the same time. 'You seem to have lost weight,' she said and then, 'Did you notice I cut my hair?

Can you make some yam fries for Miriam's birthday party on Saturday?' Everything came on fast as it always did with her. She brought me a bunch of dried grass, artificially coloured, as a peace offering.

'Girl, what did Lawal give you for your birthday?'

'A toaster.'

'Men! What imagination!'

That afternoon I gained the status of godmother to her daughter, got organized into helping at a school carnival and agreed that she join us for the evening meal. Quite an achievement for one visit, I thought. It was as if I had known her all my life, in saris, wrappers, skirts, trousers, tall, short, skinny, fat. I proposed we eat out in a local rice-and-beans place before going to the carnival.

'Girl, why spend hard-earned money on a meal in the restaurant?' she asked. 'It will only go down the sewers.' She probably took the children to the market and bought them a pair of slippers each with the money. She was going to buy a sack of rice before the prices went up at Christmas. She talked about 'investing' in sugar, which meant she had found a store where she could get it cheaper. Every naira was accounted for.

It is not as if one were prepared for calamities in life simply because the traditional structures of security were absent. As alien wives we had no recourse to employer or government. We placed our faith in providence and lived from day to day just as the local women around us did.

There were too many friends to keep in contact with the year I spent away from the country. Writing to my family used up most of my emotions, and worrying about them took up the rest. Every now and then someone or something reminded me of Brenda. 'Girl, would you? . . . Could you?' It came as an absolute shock when my husband sent me an obituary cutout from the local newspaper. 'Translated to Immortality,' it said, and had a picture of youthful Emeka in his seventies' suit and tie.

The day I walked into Brenda's living room she was in a black chiffon dress, hair done up in a subdued knot, watching a video of her dead husband being lowered into the ground in an ornate box. She hugged me perfunctorily, groaned, and then went back to watching the video, dry-eyed and intense, like she didn't want to miss the details. I squirmed on the sofa beside her and waited. 'Doesn't Daddy look nice in his suit?' she commented.

If he had died after an illness it would have been better, she said. She flicked out a roll of lavatory paper from her handbag, tore off a piece and wiped her nose. It was, as they say, A Ghastly Motor Accident. Brenda had chased out all the relatives who had come to have a satisfying mourning period according to custom. In the bedrooms the women lay, she said, in crumpled wrappers and head-ties. When the coast was clear they brought out the basin of *jollof* rice from under the bed, heaped it on plastic plates and gorged themselves. They washed it down with mineral drinks. Energies replenished, they assumed the posture of Irreparable Loss and Grieving.

This is a tragedy, Brenda had screamed at them, not a celebration. She was not going to allow for a 'decent' wait-before-the-funeral. She had slung the handbag over her shoulder, tied a black wrapper on and said she was going to shop for a coffin. The women had fallen over her and restrained her.

'Madam, take it easy,' they had pleaded. 'This sort of thing is not done. We will take care of it.'

'He was our brother,' said a distant cousin with an eye on the Mercedes Benz parked outside.

Brenda had taken the money out of her handbag and given it to a friend. The coffin was purchased and buses were hired so that all the relatives and friends could travel east to Emeka's hometown for the funeral. Brenda had locked up the house and car and released the dogs in the yard. 'You see these children,' she had said to the relatives, pointing to her young ones. 'If the man has left anything, it is for these children. So don't worry yourselves hoping for a share in it.'

There had been disputes in the village. The Catholic priest maintained Emeka had to be buried in the churchyard. Brenda had made up her mind that he was going to be buried beside the only house he had built in his lifetime, the shell of a mud-brick house in the village. She had threatened to take the corpse back to the city if the church did not cooperate. There were mutterings around her. Women gathered in corners and whispered. She had ignored them. 'When I married my husband overseas I didn't see any of you,' she told them. 'You are not going to be the ones to tell me where to bury him.'

Finally she had abandoned the Catholic Church, got a local Igbo priest in his white robes, with his white-robed companions, to officiate at the funeral ceremony. The Igbo brother from the charismatic sect wished to give Brenda her money's worth—he beat his gong and danced around the casket, chanting. The children were lined up on chairs in the front. Behind them sat Brenda's friends. The relatives and village people had stood at the back, still murmuring. They seemed to be afraid of her. Brenda sat taut and waited, wiping the sweat off her forehead. An hour, half an hour, fifteen minutes to go and the man would be buried and there would be peace. She had carried it out this far. She had to see the whole thing through and then leave this village.

Brenda looked so charming in her purple blouse with gold buttons, her ears pierced in three places and three sets of gold rings adorning each of her earlobes. Four months had gone by since we had last met. 'If it weren't for God I couldn't have bounced back,' she declared cheerfully, squinting in the February sunshine. 'A relationship with God. That is the important thing. If I didn't have this longstanding relationship I would have despaired. Girl, it is lonesome without a husband. A whole new ball game, as the Americans say. Even if the man wasn't doing anything at least there was the security that you were his wife and he was there. If you were sick in hospital he would come in and say, "What's going on, how's my wife?" Now you drag yourself to hospital and drag yourself back. Every doorknob, every hinge that is faulty in the house, is your headache. This one needs school fees, that one a chemistry textbook. You buy rice, yams, *garri*. You pay every blessed bill. I tell you, girl,' she heaved, 'if it weren't for the good Lord I would have followed the man in ten days.' She got into the car and gently shut the door. 'You have to wait for the Lord. That's what the Bible says. We all have to die one day and then you either meet Him as your judge or your king. I tell you, I want to stay on His right side, girl. If you don't know God you don't know where you're going. You turn over and die like a chicken. I know exactly where Emeka is . . . What are you doing on Saturday? I'm running short of kerosene. Let's join the queue at the Mobil station and then maybe look for some flour to buy. You don't have some to spare, do you? I have this idea of making coconut bread to sell . . .'

She left me standing there as the Mercedes Benz pulled out smoothly and was gone.

greener pastures

I must have dozed off as we passed the little villages, the huts shaped like huge umbrellas resting on the ground. I marvelled at the way the thatched roofs ballooned out in perfectly conical shapes and sat gracefully, with just strips of the mud walls showing. The mango trees were weighed down with that huge variety of mangoes, each succulent fruit a meal in itself.

When I woke up next, the round huts and mangoes had been left behind. This was rectangular country. I mused over an anxious student's research into the 'curvilinear' African culture. There was nothing curvilinear or circumferential about this part of the country. Rectangular mud-houses with thatched or zinc roofs were tucked away amongst bananas, palms and other dense foliage. The women carried basins of yams just harvested on their heads; the men, the occasional radio or water cooler. Everything was balanced effortlessly on their heads. There was a church every few kilometres proclaiming salvation, also a rectangular mud-structure with a corrugated iron roof, distinct with its crooked spire and iron cross at the top.

It was the green, and the late-afternoon sunlight on it, that made me squint. The road wound around gently rolling hills of green, the terraced slopes covered with rubber and palm trees. They were private estates, plantations in neat symmetrical rows that disappeared into a green glow in the distance. I had no idea how far we were from the coastal town, Calabar. The milestones were buried under the tapering anthills and the grass that grew tall and lush by the roadside.

I met the Americans in the petrol station where we got off the taxi to stretch our feet, having been packed six to the back seat. Jim and Bryan hopped about looking for the washroom. 'Head for the bush, my friend,' said my fellow traveller, 'the nearest hotel is in Calabar.' It was late evening when the taxi driver dropped me off at the centre of the city, at a motor-park that was being rapidly cleared of travellers and touts.

'Anything to eat around here?' I asked.

'They eat snails and periwinkles here,' the taxi driver said, 'and leaves and things.'

I had a strange sense of adventure and discovery, a feeling that the place was waiting to be explored.

The easiest thing to do would have been to check into one of the hotels—the Hilton, the Metropolitan or the Sea View Hotel—and enjoy the comforts of a musty, carpeted room, a cosy bed, and a crackling television set, complete with a quasi-European menu. But I chose to look for the lady I had been given an introduction to, in the hope of finding hospitality there, before I ventured out in the morning. The lady in question, I was told, was a curator in the local museum, a widely travelled and enlightened woman of some distinction.

'She'll put you up for any number of nights. We were schoolmates in Benin. Just mention the fact that you are my colleague,' my professor at work had said casually.

I located her place with some difficulty, opened the
formidable gate as noiselessly as possible, and entered keeping
an eye out for dogs. It was a large two-storied suburban house
with ornate windows that lined the front, facing the gate. All
the windows were shut. The veranda was choked with tropical
greenery, azaleas, ferns, ivy, and other plants that spilt out,
spread, and trailed about the place. A man emerged out of the
shadows of the veranda when he saw me. He was short, wore
a sleeveless vest, and had a cigarette between his fingers. I
introduced myself and stated the purpose of my visit, shifting
my travelling bag from one shoulder to the other.

'O, no problem,' he said, sizing me up, 'Francis is an old
friend. You can stay here . . . Let me call my wife.' He opened
the living room door, then shut it after I entered, bolting
it at the top and bottom. He then disappeared behind an
inner door.

It was a red room by any description—red wall-to-wall
carpeting, red mock-velvet chairs and settee. A poster
framed in glass said JESUS and had enormous dollops of
blood dripping from it, red, naturally. I looked for clues to
the curator—heavy damask curtains in wine red, a surrealist
painting, which, if you stared at it long enough, sucked
you into an eddy of infinite subterranean swirls. A single
photograph on the wall showed a man in a three-piece suit,
a woman in formal evening dress and hat, and a sad-looking
child in white christening dress, entirely colonial down to
the gloves and hat and that semi-European family pose. The
stillness disturbed me.

The inner door opened suddenly and the curator appeared,
a plump woman with Afro hair and thick lenses, a sack of a
dress hanging unevenly about her. Her husband followed her,

puffing at the cigarette stub. She looked visibly confused as she sat down beside me on the settee and said, 'Yes?'

'Good evening. I'm here for an interview with the philosophy department at the university. I am from Kano . . . Professor Okoh said you were classmates in Benin.' I swallowed the tail end of my introductory speech on seeing the curator's face framed by those thick lenses at close quarters.

'Steve, did you tell her about the Sea View Hotel?'

'Flora, what about the room upstairs, just for tonight? Francis has sent her to us.'

'I'm sorry, the house is full at the moment. We have guests. And there are no spare beds in the children's room. Steve, what about the Metropolitan?'

'Flora, she can stay in the guest room, can't she?'

By this time the curator's breathing was getting laboured. I couldn't get a word in. In that ill-lit room, her glance shifted from her husband to me, straining through those lenses to detect any associations, unspoken intimacies.

'I'm sorry to intrude on you,' I cut in eventually. 'I thought I'd just get some information from you. I haven't been in this part of the country before.'

'Do you have a letter of introduction?'

'No . . . I . . . maybe you should tell me how to get to the Metropolitan . . .'

'Flora, we can't send her into town at this hour. What about the guest room?' the man persisted.

'Excuse me,' said the curator, and strode off through the inner door, her husband muttering after her.

I debated very quickly whether I should await their verdict, the outcome of their domestic quarrel. The blood and gore on the poster and the iridescent glow from the painting sent shivers through me. I rapidly unbolted the front door, top and bottom, and fled into the warm night streets of Calabar.

The Americans—they were probably sitting around with cans of beer on the terrace of one of the big hotels, getting a taste of local life. I did find them in the university the following day enquiring about places of interest. My visit to Calabar would have been one of those official trips punctuated by hotel bills, mileage on the road, and meal receipts, if it weren't for Padmini Gopalan.

The moment I met Padmini in her sparsely furnished office at the university, I knew I had a story waiting for me. A shapely lady in her fifties, she was not overly enthusiastic about meeting a stranger either, but I detected a hint of warmth behind that formal uncommunicative exterior. She was of average height, but her erect posture gave me the impression of her being tall. She wore a long, printed dress, gathered and fitted at her bust. Her hair was luxuriant, streaked with grey, and hung loose down to her shoulders. She wore a hint of eye make-up, a mere touch of lipstick, and her olive skin glowed.

'Are you Indian or Sri Lankan?' I enquired.

'It's all the same, my dear,' she said. 'We are all from the same region.'

She gave me elaborate directions to get to her place. You were to go off the major road, down several byways and alleyways, past the pineapple seller, the little park, and the Rosicrucian temple before you arrived at where she lived. I was to be there at 5 o'clock in the afternoon. She warned me that she was a vegetarian, that she hadn't done her grocery shopping and couldn't provide me any food, but I could have as many cups of tea and coffee as I liked, and a place to sleep on her settee in the living room.

I looked out for a bungalow picturesquely surrounded by jacarandas, past the pineapple stall, the thatch-roofed shop that sold milk, sugar and teabags (where I picked up a tin of coffee), and her directions led me to an obscure little house hidden from view amongst the larger houses on the avenue.

Through the gap in the window louvres I could see her in the living room with a plate on her knee. She seemed to be singing while she ate. I knocked, rattled and banged on the door before she opened it.

'I was reciting my *japa*,' she said. 'I have to listen to my devotional songs for half an hour, morning and evening. Come, come, sit down.' Then she turned up the cassette player. It was a faulty piece of equipment that crackled and spurted the devotional songs—'Ha . . . re R . . . ama, Ha . . . re Kr . . . ishna, Krishna Krishna, Ha . . . re Raa . . . ma.' She put her plate of rice and dal on the stool, stood up with palms joined, closed her eyes and did a devotional dance about the room. The crackle in the cassette player didn't seem to distract her. Incense from the dining-room table filled the room with a sickly sweet fragrance. It was time for the evening news, she said quite suddenly—midway through this ritual—and turned on the television set. There was a racket like the local freight train thundering past when the television came on.

'My son has promised to get this fixed when he comes back from Lagos,' she shouted at the top of her voice. While the television announced disjointedly the news of the commissioner's visit to the local brick factory and the 'Hare Rama Hare Krishna' grew hypnotic and repetitive, she did her peaceful little waltz, giving me a lecture at the same time on the importance of devotional music in Hindu worship.

It was a conventional, what you may call Civil Servants' Quarters, in the Government Residential Area, but the inside of the house showed signs of desultory maintenance—missing floor tiles, broken louvres on the windows, patched up with wooden boards to keep the rain out. She had a towel draped across the window to dry. Colourful pictures of Shiva and Shakti, Krishna and Radha seemed to have been cut out of Indian calendars and pasted on the walls with masking tape. Miniature Hindu deities and brass temple carvings stood on the sideboard alongside Cameroonian masks and Nigerian pottery. Curtains that had seen several seasons of repeated washing hung in strips across the windows and the front door. But it was obvious that it was the home of a scholar. Bookshelves sagged under the weight of Hindu philosophy, Jungian psychology, and fiction from Henry Fielding to Thomas Pynchon. The dining table was her desk, it appeared—it was covered with papers and books and work in progress. She was a writer, critic and translator. A bespotted old refrigerator hummed in the corner, standing on three legs.

She had mentioned her son so casually, my curiosity got the better of me. 'Yes, yes, my son . . . he is twenty-nine. He has finished his doctorate, and they have employed him as a lecturer in the anthropology department. He wrote the best thesis in the university over the past ten years . . . even the vice chancellor congratulated him personally.'

She finished her rice and dal and said, 'Let me get you coffee . . . we have the rest of the evening to talk.'

When she walked, she measured her steps with the grace of a classical dancer. I heard her in the kitchen while I browsed through her bookshelves.

'My son—everybody loves him,' she said, putting the mug of coffee down on the stool beside me. 'He doesn't smoke or drink, and they say he is not a womanizer. But you know, he is twenty-nine—he is restless and lonely. I want to take him to India next year and look out for a suitable match for him.'

'This is my side of the table,' she continued, pointing to an untidy pile of papers on the dining table. 'My son works on the other side . . . He has read all my books . . . it's a legacy I have passed on to him.'

Her eyes shone as she talked about her son, a gem among the wayward delinquents of the postmodern condition. She was in her element when we talked about books. We discussed magical realism, feminist aesthetics, and archetypal myths in Hinduism. She saw herself in terms of the chakras in Tantric philosophy, the lotus flowers of one's sensations. She maintained that her lotuses blossomed from the waist upwards, the most active part of her anatomy being her brain. 'These are all my publications,' she said, pointing to one area of her bookshelf. I stood up to examine them—there was an amazing collection of criticism, translations from Sanskrit, children's books, and chapters in scholarly works. She sipped her coffee and was lost in thought.

'More coffee? Let me bring you some fruit. It's nice to have someone to talk to, particularly someone who understands the inner workings of your culture.'

She retired to the kitchen again and emerged with my coffee and a plastic bowl of chopped pawpaw and mangoes. She had hastily sprinkled sugar over the top to take the edge off the sour fruit.

'Don't you eat meat at all?' I enquired.

'No, no, no. Meat reduces your sensitivity—killing animals

and things. You accumulate negative karma, and then you have to work it off . . . My son . . . he likes fish, prawns . . . he loves chicken. But I . . . I can do without all that. They tell me meat tastes the same . . . any kind of meat. But vegetables, each has a different flavour . . . each has a different property and function.'

I steered the conversation to her family again. 'Let me show you the album,' she said, as she went down the corridor to her bedroom. When she came back, we settled ourselves on the settee with the albums and boxes of loose photographs. There was a sudden electricity cut.

The Americans moved from one hotel to the next. They had proper sit-down meals, sausages and eggs for breakfast. They took rides on motorboats, around the swamps, at exorbitant prices. They bought black-market petrol and wood-carvings, ate pineapple and cashew fruit, and showed up at the interview looking like lobsters on the beach. 'Nice town, this,' said Jim.

Padmini groped around the dining room and found a couple of candles and a box of matches on top of the three-legged refrigerator. She lit a candle and put it on the coffee table in front of us. She opened the album with reverence.

'I haven't looked at these pictures in years,' she said. Page after page of black-and-white photographs, her life story, unfolded before my eyes. I had a feeling of awe, as if I had been given access to privileged information.

Here were stunning profiles of Padmini as a young woman of twenty-four, shiny black hair down to her waist, fine features, the refined and sophisticated look of a Moghul princess. She was photographed with her sisters, Leela and Sujatha. This was followed by pictures of her college days, the intercollegiate debates, awards and accolades. Then came marriage, her husband, tall and handsome in *jibbah* and pyjamas, as if he had stepped straight out of the silver screen of the Indian cinema. There were photographs of family picnics, with their son first, and then—'this is my daughter, Priya.'

The remark had been dropped so casually, like the glitch on the television screen. I turned and looked at Padmini. She seemed to be far away. The pages that followed had yellowing photographs of children at various stages of growth and innocence. 'Priya was a lovely baby. She looked a lot like her father.' Padmini commented on the quality of the pictures, the sunlight captured on Priya's tender features, the chiaroscuro effect on the photograph of the mother rocking her daughter to sleep. The children grew more and more attractive on each page.

And then, quite abruptly, or so it seemed, Padmini was a middle-aged woman holidaying with her young son in Cairo, Alexandria, Barcelona, Verona, and Yorkshire. She was a keen traveller. She recalled details of her visit to the Scottish lochs, Emily Brontë's home, and the Italian eighteenth-century style gardens. She was a career woman, hair cut short, spectacles and a professional look about her. There were photographs of her at the Commonwealth Literature Conference in Jamaica, in the company of Raja Rao and V.S. Naipaul.

It was as if her daughter had ceased to exist at the age of twelve. The pretty girl in Indian salwar and kameez, flinging her pigtails back with abandon, faded out of the photograph album. So did the tall film-star of a husband who had stood poised with his glass of wine at parties. He was nowhere to be seen. I didn't want to jump to conclusions. I nudged her gently with the right questions. It was as if she had been mesmerized on seeing those photographs.

Padmini and Vinod moved in with the joint family and set up house in that three-roomed Bombay flat on the fourteenth floor. Padmini was then a junior lecturer in English in a provincial college in the centre of Bombay. Vinod's mother, Ammaji, ruled the roost, dictated the menu, and supervised the general running of the house. Padmini would be up in the kitchen till late at night. Standing under the forty-watt bulb, her Introduction to Prose Fiction notes propped up against the wall at the sink, she would chop the beans finely, shell the peas, grate the coconut, and put them all in storage containers in the refrigerator. That way it would be a lot easier to start the cooking in the morning. After the children had been washed and fed in the morning, Padmini packed their lunch—chapatis and vegetable curry—in little stainless-steel tiffin boxes. Then she and her husband would be off on their Vespa scooter to join the thousands of wage-earners who poured into the streets of Bombay on foot, on buses and auto-rickshaws, and smart little Maruti cars. She looked forward to Saturdays, when she could stand in front of the mirror for the extra half hour. Then Vinod would pick her up from outside the college gates at 1 o'clock, and they would have lunch in a little south Indian restaurant around the corner from the college. Vinod would speed off on his scooter to see his friends, while Padmini sauntered around the shopping arcades and spent the rest of the afternoon, hair under the dryer, being manicured, pedicured, and having her eyebrows plucked and shaped while she read *Femina* and *Star and Style.* She would emerge fresh as a rose at 5 o'clock and take a bus home to the flat.

She talked endlessly those days; she expressed opinions, passed judgements, turned herself inside out. There was nothing in the world she wished to hide from Vinod. He was not a great talker, but he listened keenly, intently. His disapproval came in smirks and sniggers rather than harsh outbursts, but she was largely insensitive to it. She even left the letters she received on the dining table so he could read them. They lay untouched. He didn't want to know her secrets and hang-ups. He kept things to himself except for the essential talk that kept the wheels of marriage moving. His little private thoughts grew to larger ones, and, after a few years, to betrayals and infidelities. By this time Padmini had stopped talking as well and had begun to direct her energies into the Vedas. She vowed she would light a hundred diyas in the Ganesha temple. When she had carried out that vow, her mother suggested the hill temple at Tirupati. The deity there stood thirty feet tall and was known to be the most potent. Padmini dipped herself in the icy waters of the temple tank at 5 o'clock in the morning and, with her wet sari clinging to her, rolled around the outer courts of the temple, chanting the mantras along with the other pilgrims until they arrived at the feet of the formidable-looking stone figure of Lord Venkata. Things didn't seem to get better. Vinod stayed out till the early hours of the morning.

Then came the job offer from Nigeria—had Lord Venkata opened his third eye and acknowledged her sacrificial offerings? Vinod had no objections. She was a liberated woman, he claimed, and could make career decisions for herself. Her son was to go with her, but Priya had to stay behind and complete her studies at high school. That was how Priya had slipped through her fingers and was lost forever. Barely sixteen and enchantingly beautiful, in the prolonged absence of her mother, Priya was lured away into the arms of a street musician—Padmini winced as she mentioned this. He was not a classical singer well-versed in the ancient arts. This was a man who, to the accompaniment of an electric guitar, sang Elvis Presley lyrics and had the college girls enthralled on Saturday nights.

'It is her life—she still lives with him,' she concluded, as the bitterness came in huge waves and engulfed her. 'They have one child, a girl. I don't visit them . . . it is the sins of her previous birth, her karma. We can't do anything about it.'

There seemed to be an iceberg of regrets submerged beneath that calm and unruffled exterior. We sat in silence, unaware that at some stage the lights had come on again; the candle had burnt down to a mere stub. 'Let me show you the house,' Padmini said, springing up, 'so you can get ready to go to bed.'

We walked down the dismal corridor at the end of which was her bedroom. A small bathroom was to the left of the corridor. She turned into the room on the right. 'This is my son's room,' she said, smoothing down the bedspread on his bed. It was not the room of a twenty-nine-year-old anthropologist but rather that of an overgrown schoolboy. Arnold Schwarzenegger flexed his triceps and Clint Eastwood squinted from the walls. The doors of the wardrobe were covered with pictures of pop stars.

'Everybody loves him . . . my son . . . but he is missing his culture,' Padmini reiterated.

To me it seemed as if her son wasn't doing too badly with culture substitutes. There was something stark about the room, in spite of the anthropologist's attempts at livening it up with his movie idols. The cement floor was chilly and bleak.

I settled myself on the couch in the living room with cushions and a blanket, half conscious of the rain lashing against the window panes as I fell asleep. Ocean smells filled the night air of my dreams. I was momentarily spirited back to a south Indian bazaar, where film music blared out of the loudspeakers and crowds of people wended their way through the stalls. Pyramids of sweets in rainbow colours decorated with silver topping, hot chickpea masala and pani-puri served on cheap china plates, heaps of jasmine and baskets of pink roses ready to be made up into garlands . . . Padmini shook me gently at 5 o'clock in the morning with a cup of coffee.

'I take forty-five minutes for my *japa* and yoga. I have to bathe before sunrise.' She disappeared down the corridor. She insisted on breakfast when she reappeared, fragrant and elegant in a pale-blue cotton sari and white blouse.

I followed her into the tiny kitchen. There was a small black kerosene stove on a cement platform and three misshapen aluminium saucepans beside it. In the corner were a few empty beer bottles. A kitchen knife and odd bits of cutlery lay in a rack beside the stove.

'I live really rough out here,' she said with a self-conscious air, 'no time to polish the silver or arrange flowers in vases.'

'I have no business asking this, but I'm curious,' I said. 'What are your plans for when your son gets married?'

'I can't live alone . . . and all the good men are either married or dead.' Almost as an afterthought, she added, 'You can't be lonely when you can read and write.' I could see her fifteen years on, in the hushed stillness of an ashram, erect and trim in her saffron robes, meditating in the lotus position.

'My son will be back tomorrow,' she said, as I boarded the taxi that was to take me to the motor-park. 'He gets anxious about me.'

borrowed feathers

'That was most uncharacteristic of me!' thought Sophie. She was not the kind that confronted a woman on the street or picked a quarrel unnecessarily. She was the type that blended with the colour of the carpet. She liked to be left alone. She could never find the suitable words to return an insult or an unjust abuse. Most of the time things bubbled inside her as hurt and spilt out on paper in retrospect. She could think of ever so many occasions when the reasonable thing to do would have been to give a stinging slap, or ask to have the car pulled up, and get off in a huff in the middle of nowhere. Not Sophie. She had let things pass time after time, swallowed it all, seen things in perspective and in relief—the goldfish in the glass jar would have done better. Of course, all the things she should have said and done enacted themselves in her mind for weeks afterwards. But she could never have said them. The simple truth is she dreaded a row, a scene, where wives hitch up their wrappers and spoil for a fight. In public! She hated advertising her misery and preferred to deal with it in the quiet of early mornings, alone in her study, when the family was asleep.

Sophie had a lousy track record in belligerent verbal exchanges with women whose motives were suspect. There were stories of beer bottles and coat hangers being broken over men's heads in attempts by wives to establish territorial rights. That was completely beyond her pale.

'We missed you,' said a kindly neighbour-lady, on Sophie's return home from a two-month holiday.

'Who are we, you and him?' she wished to ask. She barely knew the woman.

'We enjoyed the maize from your farm in your absence,' the woman added provocatively.

'What else did you enjoy in my absence?' she thought to ask.

'The house was too big for him . . .,' the woman said, 'with you being gone.' Thoughts arranged themselves into words unspoken. 'Praise the Lord, you're back.'

'She's a very kind woman,' Sophie's husband had said warmly, 'She brought us pepper soup and took care of the children.' But that is another story.

'How did she make me do something so uncharacteristic?' Sophie cringed, 'And how did I do it?' Her inside voice told her that the woman in question might use her mother-in-law's visit as an excuse to let herself into her house—a dish of pounded yam and palm kernel soup as a sign of hospitality from the town dweller to Mamma from the village. If they ran into each other, she would try to pass it off as a friendly encounter, the strumpet! The very thought of dealing with a situation like that was unpleasant.

'Is it a woman with sallow skin and arched eyebrows swinging her hips down a bumpy dirt road that is going to change my fortune?' Sophie reassured herself. 'That is how they enter your life, your world, when you least suspect it,' said the inner voice again.

Kole was usually very discreet, to the point that Sophie always ended up giving him the benefit of the doubt. He looked trampled all over when his loyalty was called into question, so morally outraged, that it was Sophie who apologized first. Somehow things had gone awry this time. He got her schedule wrong that morning; otherwise, the unusual meeting would not have taken place. He allowed a cautious margin for Sophie to have left home for work, before arranging for the woman to arrive at his house, in his car. She was grandly seated beside the driver, making small talk as they approached the street.

Sophie and the driver crossed each other 100 yards from the house. Smart guy, the driver. He sensed danger when Sophie pulled up. Who's the woman, she asked, still at the wheel, even though she had noticed at a glance who the passenger in her husband's car was. The woman with the green wrapper and head-tie tried to look the other way to avoid being identified. The driver attempted to cover up for the master, caught in a situation he did not care to be in. It's a woman I picked up on the road, Madam, he stuttered, she wanted me to drop her there. Where? There, he insisted, pointing to a general direction away from Sophie's house.

The woman, in the meantime, realized she couldn't sit in the car and pretend to be a wayside rock any longer. She got out awkwardly and came towards Sophie, swinging her hips and adjusting her head-tie. The dreaded moment.

'Good morning, Madam,' she greeted with nauseating familiarity.

'Who's this?' Sophie asked the driver, pointing to her. 'Where are you taking this woman to?' That was how it all began. Drumbeat and war rhetoric. The battle lines were drawn. It was as if she had slipped into the role of many a wronged woman describing similar situations. All things totally out of character came tumbling out of her mouth. She was beginning to enjoy this act. She was standing apart and watching herself, this tough woman, wife, the rightful owner of home and husband, rough-handling this fool of a mistress caught in the act. She might as well have been, anyway.

'Madam, don't you know me? I am the one . . .,' whimpered the ridiculous-looking gap-toothed woman.

'I wouldn't know you even if you told me,' Sophie thundered. 'I only know you as the woman who hangs about my husband's office.'

'Madam, I go there just to phone my sister. You know me, I used to work for . . .'

'Is it a public phone or are you his responsibility?' Sophie stormed at her, and then to the driver, 'Take this woman where you picked her up from and drop her there. She can go and sit in my husband's office if she likes. But she is not entering my house.' Sophie had never shown such firmness before, putting her foot down and all.

'Madam, it's not like that. Not like that, Madam,' the driver pleaded, getting very uncomfortable.

'Why is she sneaking up to my house knowing I'll be at work?' Sophie asked, obliquely. 'If she is a decent woman, she would have come in the evening with her husband. Kole got his timing wrong, didn't he?'

'Madam, you surprise me . . .' The woman tried to sound wounded.

'You surprise me too,' Sophie taunted. 'A married woman like you . . .,' she was getting carried away with the sanctity of marriage.

'I'll come to your house in the evening if you like, with my son . . . I don't know what people have been saying to you.' The woman was persistent.

'There's no need,' Sophie cut in. 'One warning is enough for the wise.' Now where did I hear that, she asked herself next. It must have come from one of my experienced-in-betrayal friends, she concluded. She thought of adding something about the malignant python who was slow in movement but deadly in action. What that epithet might have landed her in, she wasn't sure of. Halfway through this exchange, seeing this pathetic, pleading woman, this vulture beaten by the rain, her knees began to buckle. Have I barked up the wrong tree, she wondered. Should I soften up a bit and just sound generally outraged, she pondered. She decided against it. Her words took on a life of their own and twisted themselves into odd shapes. Moreover, she was beginning to gain an audience—the newspaper vendor, the woman frying yam slices on the kerb, the boy on the bicycle and the roadside mechanic.

'Madam, let me explain . . .' The woman clung to the car door.

'Why are you shouting like a tethered she-goat in labour? Sophie was loud. Her voice was not her own. She had never seen a she-goat in labour. Now, where did that come from? It must have been Jacintha's legacy. Jacintha, full of bravado, challenging her husband, her lifelong adversary to a continual verbal combat in which she always took the lead, having rehearsed the lines previously. When he had had enough of her he'd say: 'I'll marry five wives. Mark my words. When I get tired of one, I'll send her away and marry another one.'

'That's where you're wrong,' Jacintha'd reply. 'You've just married your fifth wife. I'm your first and fifth wife. I'm going nowhere, not to talk of sweeping me out of the house with a broom.'

The woman still stood by the side of the car appealing for the facts to be set right.

'I've nothing to say to you. I don't like confrontations like this,' Sophie confessed, slipping back into her skin, 'I'm not used to it. Only friends and relatives can come to my house. You are neither a friend nor a relative. So, what is your business there?'

Echoes in her brain. Now, who said that? It must have been wisdom inherited from sister-in-law Charity in Lagos. She had always been a smart talker. She made impromptu speeches full of womanly astuteness to her husband's real and imagined mistresses, and then repeated them to Sophie later, when narrating the story, in the exact tenor of voice. She, of course, had imbibed the art from Kole's mother who spoke pure poetry when provoked. The imagery alone was enough to drive any woman of dubious status, miles from the scene, never to return. She could strip you naked with her words in the middle of the street when you are fully clothed! She could cut you down to unrecognizable shreds when the timing was right. She could bowl you over with a conundrum.

'Your lifestyle is different from mine,' Sophie continued, still angry, as the woman squeezed herself beside her in the car, pleading for reconciliation, 'so stay where you are and don't cross my path. If you like, hang out at my husband's office until he shows you the door. But don't let me catch you anywhere near my place.' She was running out of things to say. A woman who is a public well, she thought of saying, will soon dry up. If you bring ant-ridden firewood to your house, you'll surely be visited by lizards. Sophie shifted gears and drove the car like a maniac. She hardly knew this woman beyond what extended-family gossip had presented to her.

'I don't want to quarrel with you, Madam.' The woman kneaded her fingers. 'I'll continue to greet you when I see you, because you are *our* wife.' Sophie flew into a rage again on being reduced to a communal spouse.

'Do what you like—if you haven't seen a *bature* wife before, let me show you. Now, get out of my car.' Sophie pulled up at the side of the road, a long way from her home and let the woman out. The crunch of the kola nut may be 'sweet' to the hearer but it is the woman with the stained mouth who knows the taste.

Sophie's words reverberated in her mind as she drove off, and sounded empty and hollow in recall. She knew that she didn't own the house or her husband's body or soul. The inalienable right of a wife was something her friends propped themselves up with, it was more evident in their speech and manner than in the privileges they enjoyed. Over a period of twenty years, Sophie had learnt to let go of things one by one, possessions, privacy, husband, marriage. They all took on different meanings in her adopted culture. So how did she allow herself to be drawn into this confrontation?

She didn't have the facility with language either, that her husband's people did. Theirs was richly imagined, vivid in colour and texture. She heard birds calling, she felt the quiver of shattering glass, she heard the sound of a motorbike on a hot, dusty road in the rhythmic inflection of their voices. When Kole talked to his mother, the gentle cadences resonated with caressing tenderness. It was the same language that he used to distance her, his wife. The English language sat uneasily on his tongue and temper. It gave him a perpetual frown on his face, and an abrupt manner. For him, there were no endearments in the English language. He said the minimum, and that was spoken without emotion.

Every married woman is sitting on a six-inch nail, Kole's mother once said. It is when she raises her bottom that you discover the problem. A local wife might announce her agony to the world and call for a family meeting, or she might sit tight-lipped hoping for divine intervention to bring her relief. Not that Mamma had it easy in her own day either. She had to cook special meals with smoked bush-meat and fish, the day her husband's woman came to visit. Then she would clean the compound and fetch water from the well for her bath. She rolled out the mat on the kitchen floor and retired for the night, while the woman with gleaming camwood-stained skin and cheap perfume took herself to the inner room to share the 'iron bed' with the man of the house. These women belonged to a class, Mamma said, probably the class of household trash. It didn't take Mamma more than five minutes to judge character. The world to her was divided into simple black and white, the wicked and the generous, wives and harlots. If you bump into a tree once, you bend down when you go under it the next time. The one-eyed man is king in the country of blind people.

'Why didn't I remember to use any of these aphorisms,' Sophie wondered, 'on my last, unpleasant encounter?'

the white rooster

He tossed from one side to the next; he sighed, he got up and rummaged in the plastic box for tablets for a headache and nerves. I lay on the same bed watching him in the dark. The luminous hands of the alarm clock pointed eerily to 4 o'clock. When he turned the radio on, I got out of bed. There wasn't much I could do for him. His beloved was dying and he was grieving for her—on my bed.

It is like a video-strip in my mind, that Easter weekend when I first discovered I was sharing him with someone else. You put yourself in the right mood for misery and the whole thing comes back, complete with the colour of her wrapper, the nylon scarf and the tribal marks on her cheeks.

The job down south had been a turning point in our marriage, a detour, a bypass, a pleasant diversion for him in unfamiliar territory. He was to live away from me and the children for two years. I had discouraged him from going, I had thrown tantrums, wept, created a scene in the presence of his close friends. But he was determined, in his grim, tight-lipped manner. That was the beginning of our separate lives, for him a new lease of bachelorhood and the privilege of being alone after sixteen years of marriage, for me, feelings of despair, rejection and incompleteness in a foreign culture.

He came every Friday evening though, after sundown, and left before sunrise on the Monday morning. It was also the beginning of his life as a travelling husband and of all the trappings that go with it.

I lay awake at nights and wondered if he was cut out to be single like some people are. I called him my 'silent Buddha', my 'sadhu', my 'Buddhist monk', sometimes, as he sat in the living room lost in thought, coiling a single strand of hair around his finger. He doubted like Graham Greene. Surely that Genesis story was a myth like all the other creation myths. Surely the Earth, being one of the numerous planets in the universe, was not the only privileged one. Why didn't God make us perfect in the first place? Why the Fall? Why the test? Did God fear competition from man? What is sin anyway? Is it not a societal, cultural phenomenon?

When he moved away from us, he chose an austere existence in a three-roomed house standing crookedly on sandy soil with a single mango tree in the yard. Lizards chased each other over the cement steps leading to his place. The heat beat down with a vengeance on the corrugated zinc roof. The river was only minutes away, an enormous sheet of glass as far as the horizon, but you had to go up the slope on the road to see it. The place had neither water in the taps nor electricity. A metal water-tank sat precariously on a cement platform outside his front door. He used candles, and sometimes sat in the dark with his radio on.

'I have no emotion left for pets,' he declared once, when the children wanted to bring the dog into the house. Dogs had to be chained and kept in their place, strictly for guarding the house. Where were his emotions, I wondered, if he had any at all. His grandmother, with whom he had spent his early childhood in the village, found use for a child only when she needed firewood, or water from the stream. 'As far back as I can remember,' he would reprimand our private-school-trained, urban children, 'I did everything for myself.' To me, it sounded like something from the previous century—the boy from the village going to school in town, with his mat rolled up and his steel trunk on his head. Where was I? I wondered, as he walked miles to school from the railway station, in his khaki shorts, holding his Cortina shoes in one hand. They pinched. By the time he was ten years old, he had dispensed with everyone around him—he was completely capable of looking after himself. It is that self-same boy in the faded photograph that I saw in him now—tough, resilient and independent even of a God.

I was made to be part of a team, conditioned for marriage and for a life which venerated the husband. My Indian heritage kept my grandmother behind the steel almirah when she spoke to my grandfather. My mother had had her marriage arranged for her at seventeen, and derived her life's satisfaction from watching my father eat his meals, and caring for his needs to the minutest detail.

She was a receptionist in that little private hospital tucked away among the *dogon yaro* trees at the end of a bumpy stretch of dirt road. His sister's house was right next to the hospital—a roomy house with children playing on the veranda amidst piles of washing that awaited ironing. It was here, in his sister's yard, that he would sit on steamy, hot afternoons with his glass of beer, watching the bustle outside the hospital.

They exchanged greetings as she came in for the afternoon shift. He knew she was from a neighbouring village by her accent; she spoke his language, except for those colourful phrases peculiar to her village. She helped out in his sister's house whenever she was off duty, cooking, ironing or plaiting someone's hair. She would have merged with the other invisible members of the extended family who did odd chores around the house, if it weren't for the fact that she stood out in my husband's mind.

Sometimes she would come forward to take his empty glass inside. He looked her over and enquired gently about her work, her parents, her village. She would answer in monosyllables, but she was a constant presence in his sister's house when he was around. If he didn't see her there when he stopped by after work, his eyes searched her out. Sometimes he would park his car outside the hospital and go in to greet her.

It was when my husband moved into the three-roomed house that I felt the first stirrings of unease—he would have called it jealousy. He was leading a life of his own, unaccountable to me as a partner in marriage. And what was wrong with that? I knew several commuting husbands, men who for years lived away from their families in big cities, visiting their wives and children periodically. Hannatu, Biola and my other women friends didn't brood over companionship or the lack of it, nor did they get hysterical over similar, convenient arrangements. They accepted it with grace and lived their lives to the full. They kept the household going with the help of numerous sisters, cousins and brothers-in-law, the children fed and sent to school, the vegetable patch weeded, the poultry yard swept and the Volkswagen Beetle in manageable condition. The husband arrives for a weekend and it is like Christmas! A chicken freshly slaughtered for his dinner, the pepper-soup bubbles in the pot, the house gets tidied and order is restored for forty-eight hours. He comes to a readymade home, mercifully escaping the grinding routine and the problems encountered in his absence—the malaria attacks, the pneumonia, the broken arm, the petrol queues and the electricity cuts.

With me it was never a honeymoon when he drove in on Friday evenings. I bristled with resentment. By Saturday, I loosened up a little and narrated all the trivia that had kept me going in his absence. I expected an hour-by-hour rundown of events from him. But he carefully sifted and censored and selected what he told me. I blossomed in his presence though, however brief it was. In the way he took control of things from the moment he arrived. There was a precision, a firmness, even in the way he tuned the radio. He always got the frequency and the metre-band he was looking for, clean and clear, not fuzzy and muffled as I heard it usually, with sea gulls crying in the background.

It was on one of these weekend visits that he mentioned her, very casually. He didn't single her out for mention—he remarked in passing that he would be in a real strait if it weren't for his niece and a certain Agnes who came each week to help clean his little house. He didn't have to say more—my wifely intuition determined the rest. And that is where, I presume, it all began. He sipped his beer in the living room and watched her thin frame through the open door as she dusted and lingered over the louvres, folded his dressing-gown tenderly, and made his bed. Week after week she was into the little intimate details of where he kept his toothbrush, the side of the bed he slept on, the way he hung his shirt by the collar on the corner of the wardrobe door. He watched her leave her fingerprints on everything, and as he moved about his solitary house late in the evening, he felt her lingering presence.

At Christmas and Easter, we usually accompanied him down south for a brief holiday, and we stayed in this stark and crooked house, without water and electricity. I had the uneasy feeling right from the start that my being there was an intrusion. I went about the house changing things around, putting his shirts on hangers, trying to leave my stamp where she had been. The house was spotless. The children enjoyed this place hugely. It was like camping, they said. An empty living room with two chairs, an ashtray and a little Sony pocket-radio on the dining table. His files, books, Milan Kundera and John Updike, lay scattered on the floor. The kitchen had a kerosene stove, a box of matches, one set of cutlery, a plate, a coffee mug and an aluminium kettle. No fridge. No flowers.

He went to work as usual while we were there, calling at his sister's place to see her before coming home to the little house. He was a dutiful man, my husband, and made sure he did the right thing by her, and by me. Some men are clumsy when it comes to two women, they lie, they cheat, they are so heavy-handed about it, it shows. One of the women suffers, and it is usually the wife. I suffered within but not because my husband treated me badly. Oh no! I suffered because he was so adept, because he was such an artist and because he 'loved' me in his own way. He was so careful not to hurt me that in my Anglo-Saxon-trained, Indian mind, his deception seemed doubly worse. He bought expensive presents for the children whenever we visited. He took us to the Palm Grove Restaurant where we sat under palm trees as freshly tapped palm wine was brought down from the trees and served along with peppered meat grilled on hot charcoal. He was 'bridging the cultures' admirably. He had, as they say, his act together.

I was the misfit sitting in the heart of Nigeria, donning a brightly coloured wrapper and blouse, but experiencing an irreparable loss. The Indian movies of my childhood and youth hadn't prepared me for this.

I was six years old in my purple skirt and blouse and hair plaited and tied with purple ribbons. It was my first week at school. My father was the newly posted magistrate in that town. My mother, the daughter of a wealthy landowner, was conscious of our social standing and expected me to be friendly with suitably well-dressed children at school. But the teacher came by to visit at the end of the week, and in between the coffee and the tiffin that arrived on a stainless steel tray, I heard her say to my mother: 'This child has a large heart, Ma. She is always with the poorest girl in the class, that peon's daughter who comes to school with a row of safety pins on her blouse, and no chappals . . . The child has a heart of a saint, Ma.' Where was my large heart now, and my saintly disposition?

It was when his friend Yakubu was visiting that I first heard of the white rooster. A tribal funeral rite, he explained, where at a man's death (or a woman's), all his earthly lovers presented themselves at the burial with a white rooster each. It was a ceremony discreetly carried out at the tail end of the funeral when the immediate family had left the place. But it was not without its spectators who boasted of the man's conquests or the woman's promiscuity as the case may be. Adultery, tacitly or openly accepted, got a public airing. Yakubu made a joke of it in his usual facetious way, something about the white roosters lining up to follow the man to the other world. It intrigued me though, as many of my husband's traditional rites and customs did. Why white? White that is worn by widows in India, symbolically shunning the colour and splendour of this world on the death of a husband? White that stands for unblemished bridal purity and innocence in some places? White that now signified adultery, deceit, 'the other woman'.

That Easter my uneasiness poisoned our entire visit. Not without reason though. He seemed more familiar with her than ever before, a mutual understanding that excluded suspicion and query. Agnes didn't come to clean the house while I was there. However, I did see her from time to time. With me she was polite, almost respectful, like the pubescent 'amariya' in the Hausa culture, distractingly invisible, hiding behind her nylon *gelle*. It was a little tableau in which he and she were the central characters and I, the unseen but all-knowing chorus.

I lost out on all counts. I hadn't neglected him or his household or our children. They had always been my priority. He had never complained. But I was not *her* and could never unlearn myself to be. I did all the little things that wives usually outgrow after sixteen years of marriage—gave him freshly squeezed orange juice when he came in after a game of badminton, and had his meals served on special plates, arranged flowers in vases, bought books and cards in and out of birthday seasons.

But I was not monosyllabic like her, nor servile, even when I tried to be a wholesome and cheerful chattel. My education and upbringing came through when I dusted the louvres. She was without expectation; she had him when he chose to be with her, and demanded nothing of him. When she was not in her hospital uniform and smelling of antiseptic, she was in what seemed to be her one and only faded-blue wrapper.

She didn't listen to the radio and didn't claim to know about existentialism. But she probably knew how to love.

That was eight years ago. Since then my husband resigned his job down south and has moved back with us. Every time his travels took him in that direction, my thoughts went to her. But I assuaged my fears thinking that distance would have cooled his ardour.

The grimness with which he announced her illness startled me. She was dying of an undiagnosed disease in the same hospital where she had worked. A telephone message had said she was on the decline. A cloud hung over the two of us that entire evening; he, choked with grief, tried to doze in snatches with the radio on. I tried to read a book, my head splitting with questions.

It didn't come as a surprise to me when I saw him packing his travelling case early in the morning. If there was a message for him at the office that she had died, he would travel directly, he said. The menacing white rooster rose like a spectre in my mind.

rescue-remedy

At twenty-two, Alison and Chika had discovered each other. They belonged to the generation of draft-dodgers and flower children, love with a capital L, and transcendental meditation as the cure for all ills. They quoted Betty Friedan and Germaine Greer and formed a strong sisterhood in college.

From the still backwaters of eastern Nigeria, Chika was hurled into a torrent of social causes in urban America. Alison was the open window through which she garnered these causes. Chika was roped into seminars on Indian land rights. 'They are our sisters,' Alison said of the Cherokee Indians. Chika felt no kinship with them but went along anyway to the seminars and protest marches. They demonstrated in Harvard Square against the mining of uranium in Western Australia, and against apartheid in South Africa. The Incas and the Pacific Islanders got them out on the streets, risking arrest and detention, not to mention the Vietnam war rallies. They attended all-night pop concerts in open fields, and theatre productions in barns with flagons of red wine and cheese doing the rounds. They were on the counterculture battlefront.

Alison was living with her parents at the time but Mom was adding scallops to the living-room curtains and was changing the wallpaper; the sit-down meals in the wood-panelled dining room were getting longer and stuffier and Alison decided it was time to move out. The two friends rented an apartment together, knocked up bits and pieces of furniture from rummage sales and started a new life. Professor Bennet brought them a bunch of sweet peas from the florists the day they moved house. Alison stuck it in a Thousand Island salad-dressing jar.

Alison cooked whole foods—brown rice, brown eggs, whole wheat and the like, but mostly she suggested they eat food raw. When overcome with a longing for home cooking, Chika resorted to 'pounded yam' that came out of a packet, and beans in cans. Alison said that Africans swallowed their *foofoo* because they were too lazy to chew it. She talked at length about the planet Earth and their responsibilities towards conserving its resources. Chika's mind, cramped and confined in set ways of thinking, loaded with prejudices and inhibitions, expanded and filled out like a sponge. She 'grew' and matured in Alison's company and when it was time to leave the United States, Alison saw her off at Logan International Airport, Boston. 'We'll do all those crazy things again,' she reassured her between hugs and sniffles, 'just keep visualizing me on a camel train across the Sahara.'

Alison was a faithful correspondent. The calligraphy on recycled paper was poetry from across the Atlantic. Her letters painted every nuance of feeling and emotion she had experienced. She described the trip she had taken to the Grand Canyon, she talked about her dog Hunger developing arthritis, and the pram she had purchased at a garage sale to take him for strolls along the beach. She sent Chika recipes for bulgur wheat casseroles and vegetarian enchiladas. Alison had a job with the American-Indian Welfare Department in New

Jersey, while promoting in her free time various Third World arts and crafts. Chika had, in the meantime, married and had four children over a period of ten years. The social causes of their student days now lost their edge—other pressing and more immediate problems of living and maintaining a family took their place.

Alison's letters through the nineteen eighties were full of her feminist involvements. She recommended books written by women, she supported abortion as a woman's right, and had just finished a course on self-defence—a tae kwon do routine of sorts. She gave Chika a self-affirming mantra to start the day with—'I am whole, resolute, strong, loving, giving, nurturing, illumining . . .' and so it went. One postcard came from a Caribbean coast where she was paying homage to female goddesses with other feminists. She talked about the virtues of hypnosis and homeopathy, and that the former helped sort out her past. Her father, as Chika remembered him, was a warm and cheerful person, an ex-soldier who drank heavily and swore and made racist remarks generally without realizing it. He liked Chika and always enquired of Idi Amin, and the starving millions in Ethiopia whenever they met. But Dad had become increasingly critical of Alison's political and social activities. Alison also complained of Dad's miserliness. Everything that went wrong in her life, Alison concluded, originated with Dad.

Camel train or not, Alison managed to get to Africa, and to Chika's part of the continent. 'Don't bang doors!' she said to various members of Chika's household, 'The noise level . . . I am not used to it.' She had to meditate each day in order to get through the disorganized stretch of life as she saw it in Nigeria.

'It is so hard to make meaningful conversation here,' she complained before long. 'Do people usually come to your home and then sit down and read newspapers?'

'Oh, yes, sometimes they watch television,' Chika teased, 'and we catch up on their magazines when we visit them . . . Do you usually have soul-searching discussions when your visitors come?'

'Most people in the States don't visit unless they have something to say to you.' Chika wondered how she could convey to her friend in one visit what she had taken a lifetime to learn, that visiting was often a mechanism for maintaining contact, of sharing communal space and concerns. She wished to show Alison off, as a specimen from the developed world, cocky and fearless with her destiny literally in the palm of her hand. Alison's life had been so rich and diverse and so full of shaggy-dog stories. But Alison didn't want to be paraded before the visitors.

'I'd love to spend time with your friends and acquaintances but I have only three weeks in Africa and I'd rather sit in a shack somewhere by the roadside and watch local life. How about the market, eh?'

They set out in search of local culture. They hunted the bookstores for postcards of Nigerian life that Alison could send to friends. The only ones they came up with were of the head of state in his military regalia, the concrete splendour of a five-star hotel in Abuja, and of an international airport. At the market though, they revelled in the colours and designs of the fabric, the Dutch wax prints, damask, and lace with the Mercedes Benz trademark embossed on it.

'How would you like to have razor blades going up and down your bosom?' Alison asked, fingering the wrappers.

'I'd prefer it to the broom and corkscrew,' Chika replied. Alison was fascinated by the prints—snakes and ladders, scaly fish, huge green eyes riveted from an ample behind, and feather dusters, all in bright summer colours. Alison was easygoing on local foods too. They sat out on the street, on wooden benches outside a local *bukka* and ordered rice with pepper-stew. The madam who owned the restaurant had a partiality for a hyphenated menu. A piece of cardboard nailed to the restaurant door read:

Stick-meat — ₦10
Peppered-fish — ₦8
Dough-nut — ₦5
Puff-Puff — ₦2
Chin-chin — ₦5
Egg-roll — ₦6

And so forth. Alison invariably had a tummy upset on their return home and would put herself on plain boiled rice and charcoal tablets for several days afterwards.

Chika came into the kitchen one morning and there was Alison fidgeting with the primitive gas cooker trying to turn it off as the water came to the boil. 'Good morning. Would you like some tea?' she asked cheerily, pouring the water in the teapot and swishing it around. Chika cleared the kitchen table and sat down.

Alison said she couldn't understand Chika's bondage and servitude to her husband—'You live completely under his shadow,' she said. If Chika rushed around to have the meal ready when Tunde came home from work, Alison said to her—'Why don't you have a cup of tea or a snooze? You work too. He can find himself something to eat. He won't fade away.' She was trying to assign a personhood to Chika, which she had long since relinquished in opting to be eternally 'available' to her family.

'You focus far too much on Tunde,' she continued, 'and your children, and not sufficiently on yourself. You make them the centre of everything. The burden is too weighty for Tunde to bear—it is too much for anybody. He doesn't want to be the reason for your existence. He doesn't want to be Priority Number One in your life to the extent that nothing else other than your family, matters. He doesn't want to be trapped into the role of God . . . or be incapacitated so that you can do everything for him. It is unhealthy. It's an unequal relationship.'

Chika couldn't get a word in edgeways. She had nothing to complain about concerning her marriage, or in being at the service of her husband and children, but obviously it didn't fit Alison's model of a wholesome feminist relationship.

The trip to the Yankari Game Reserve was meant to give Alison a good measure of African wildlife while affording her a chance to relax with Chika's family. Tunde checked the car, while Chika and the children packed bread, fruit and vegetables in cartons for the two days they were going to spend there. Alison was chatty and vivacious. She was growing weary of town life—this was going to be a slice of the real Africa.

The first leg of the journey was smooth for all. Alison kept the children amused with her songs and anecdotes. Trouble began when they stopped for petrol in a small town on the way. 'Can we walk around the market?' Alison asked in a tone which implied that she wasn't going to take no for an answer. Tunde had his eyes on his watch. He didn't particularly enjoy long trips with the family in tow, so his mind was set on taking them from point A to point B and bringing them back intact. There was an unspoken understanding between Chika and Tunde on this matter. Chika tried to reason with Alison that, perhaps, the market would be a better idea on the way back.

The second stretch of the journey had Alison holding a piece of tissue to her nose periodically. She put her sunglasses on, adjusted the car seat, and sank into silence the rest of the way. The children knew she was moping. They offered her drinks, which she declined. Chika drew her attention to the Fulani cows with their fantastic horns but she was ignored. They arrived at the game reserve late in the evening as the sunset spread across the horizon with a myriad colours and birds filled the air. While Chika set up house in the little cottage they had rented for the period of their stay, Alison took a book and retired to bed. She remained unsociable for most of the day following. That evening Tunde went down to the Warm Springs with the children, and Chika sat outside the cottage peeling potatoes for dinner. Daylight was fading over the brambly Savannah forest. The trees looked gaunt and spectacular as their bare branches twisted up to the skies. A pigeon brooded over a neighbouring roof and an occasional bird let out a shrill cry.

'You're afraid of him, aren't you?' Alison began, taking a seat beside Chika.

'I think I know him better than you do. I avoid disagreements that don't matter one way or another.'

'I thought you'd stand up for me. And we had discussed going to the market, remember? I have come halfway round the world and he wouldn't stop for thirty minutes at the market.'

Chika was surprised at the ease with which Alison let the tears flow. She was still under the influence of the analyst. Cry. Just let it all hang out, the analyst had counselled Alison. One had to be in touch with one's feelings, be open and honest, and not withhold anything for the sake of decorum.

On their return trip, Tunde more than made up to Alison by stopping at every country market so that she could look around. Alison would say—'Can you stop at one of those villages—let me get a picture. You know, one of those with mango trees, creeping vines on the fences, and cows and sheep grazing.' When Tunde did stop she would say, 'This is not a prosperous village, let us try another one.' They didn't find a village to match her idyllic mental picture of Third World Rural Life, so they stopped at the last village on the periphery of the city. Instantly children gathered around the car. They all wanted to be photographed. The women pounding corn in wooden mortars came up and signalled that they should be paid for having a photograph of them taken. Tunde was uneasy. He knew that people resented being goldfish in a bowl for curious visitors who might take pictures of them to distant lands.

Over the next few weeks Alison endeared herself to the family by her resourcefulness. But it was one incident that the children didn't stop talking about. Jouet, their six-month-old Alsatian puppy was usually so energetic, wagging his entire behind, and rolling on the grass with his paws in the air. But one morning he suddenly lay exhausted outside the kitchen door. The children tried to revive him with milk and biscuits first, and when that didn't work, with water and glucose to prevent dehydration. But Jouet just looked the other way and seemed to be deteriorating by the minute.

By the end of the second day, the children were frantic with worry. It was a holiday weekend and there was no vet available. When all else failed, Alison opened her handbag and brought out a turquoise Chinese silk purse. Buried inside it was a miniature jar of potent liquid, distilled from select wildflowers and herbs—'rescue-remedy', it was called. It was a life-enhancing potion, which restored the balance when things were amiss between one and the cosmos, manifested in terms of extremely stressful situations. Alison wasn't sure it would work on the puppy but she was going to give the desperate remedy a try. With great solemnity, Alice administered a drop of the potion to the half-conscious and wilted puppy as the children watched anxiously. Then she talked to the puppy quietly, reassuring him that he needed the will to live.

The next morning, when the children woke up, they were ecstatic to hear the puppy scratching at the kitchen door, asking to be let in. Alison had been nervous through the night thinking of the hopes the children had placed on the rescue-remedy. The hope was part of the healing, she said later.

Chika was somewhat wary of taking Alison to church with them on Sunday morning—it might be one place, she felt, where Alison would be a complete misfit. The congregation met in a little wooden shed that stood alongside a carpenter's workshop on one side, and a rice-and-beans restaurant on the other. It was stark and chilly inside with a low ceiling and a row of wooden benches whose legs rested periodically on the uneven cement floor. Crotons and hibiscus blooms were haphazardly stuffed into a ceramic vase and set on the pulpit. The piano hadn't been tuned for a few years and left the hymn-singers behind from time to time. Scattered among the empty benches was a motley congregation of about thirty people—the prayer requests ranged from cement contracts, availability of water and electricity to protection from armed robbers and an education system free of strikes. The twin babies cooed and crawled all over the floor while the congregation prayed. The choir, consisting of six women in gold and red *aso oke*, looked like a row of bedecked Christmas trees. The pastor, newly returned from America, called on 'guard' (God), and every time he mentioned sin, his face changed and he squirmed. A radio blared in the restaurant next door and there was a clutter of forks.

Alison didn't like to label herself as anything in particular but garnered her spirituality from varied sources. 'He's a bit wet behind the ears, isn't he?' she whispered, fixing her gaze on the pastor. 'A very sexist sermon,' she added, nudging Chika.

It was just not Alison's scene. 'What brings you here? I am worried about you,' she said. Chika was relieved to get Alison back in the car after the protracted service. 'Why did he look at me like something the cat brought in?' she asked of the pastor when he attempted a handshake.

Chika's friends were determined to arrange a romantic liaison for Alison by way of a *jollof*-rice-and-plantain lunch. Among those invited was Peter, a bachelor civil servant who was to be given a privileged introduction. Alison played the fool all afternoon when she realized some plans were afoot to trap her into a romantic arrangement. 'I'm looking for a wife,' she announced to the eager gathering, 'someone who can cook my meals, clean my place and take care of my dog.'

Peter didn't have a chance. He was short and squat, he barely reached Alison's shoulders, with a wisp of a moustache.

He came in clutching a crocodile-skin handbag, which was meant to be a gift for Alison. He asked her profound questions about her plans for the future. Chika had in the meanwhile raved about Peter's accomplishments—he certainly was not a womanizer, she had said.

'You know something,' Alison commented when the guests had left and they were clearing the dishes, 'I think that guy Peter is queer. All the other men in the room were giving off sexual vibes. It was a game, you know, but Peter showed no interest at all.'

'But Alison, you didn't give him a chance. You must have put him off completely with your clowning.'

'Good, I hoped I had.' Then she added, 'I don't want to be nice. You know what I mean? Nice people die young, of cancer or AIDS or something terrible.'

It was as if Alison's visit would not have been complete without a rendezvous at the local police station. On the eve of her departure, Chika was still driving her around with a long list of things to be photographed, souvenirs to purchase, and messages to deliver. At Alison's request she pulled up beside a market where lorries were having their rear panels painted. All kinds of religious and secular scenes were being elaborately depicted in primary colours—hunters, wild animals, an emaciated Saviour on the cross, the Last Supper, three-headed gods, and so on. They were moving tapestries that traversed the countryside, full of colour and detail. Alison jumped out of the car and adjusted her camera lens for a photograph. The next moment a policeman tapped her on the shoulder.

'Madam, can I see your papers? Why are you taking pictures of our market?'

Alison was so shocked she couldn't find the words to answer him. Chika rushed to her side. A crowd gathered around them, whispering and pointing at Alison.

From being a curious and eccentric *bature*, Alison had become a spy, the CIA, the KGB, instantly, with strange, dark designs in wanting to photograph a marketplace. Alison tried to protest, 'It's the truck . . . the beautiful truck . . .,' she said weakly.

'Don't you have beautiful trucks in your country, madam?'

'But they are different. Our trucks are long . . . made of metal . . .,' she proceeded to describe. Chika tried to defend Alison but was shoved aside.

'What is it in our market that you are trying to take pictures of? Where is your passport? Tickets?'

'Where is your ID?' Alison asked in return. The officer exploded.

'ID—Who are you to ask me for my ID? I know whom to and where I should show my ID.' With that he snatched Alison's camera and travel documents and said, 'Let's go to the police station.'

Alison and Chika looked imploringly at the crowd around them. Not one face was sympathetic. Leaving the car in the middle of the market place, they walked like two criminals behind the policeman (who had by then acquired several assistants). The crowd jeered. Alison used all the four-letter words at her command. Chika murmured the Lord's prayer and wondered frantically how she was going to get a message across to her husband. Maybe they were under arrest. Maybe they would waste away in the bowels of a local police station and nobody would know of their whereabouts.

The police station was a man's world where he could taunt, tease, insult and deride any woman who entered its grimy interior. You are guilty until you are proven innocent, it proclaimed.

On seeing the women being led in, other policemen abandoned their posts and joined the party to watch the fun. They were shoved into the far interior of the police station, into a room where the officer on duty sat at his wooden desk, chatting with petty thieves. The place stank of beer and urine.

They were directed to sit on a bench across from the officer. 'Don't worry, Madam,' he reassured Alison, 'We'll sort out this thing.'

He flipped through her passport, checked her date of birth and examined her photograph. Then he leered at her—'Why are you taking pictures of our market? Don't you have markets in your country?'

The pointless interrogation started again.

'Could I please phone my husband?' Chika asked hesitantly.

'The lines are down,' snapped the officer, 'There is no need.'

After forty minutes of cross-examination the officer said, 'Now the only way we can settle this matter is to expose this film. Then we'll know if it's the market or the truck.'

Alison was hysterical. 'My Fulani women . . . my basket-weavers . . . elephants—you're going to ruin them all. I won't have it. I want to report you. You have no right to harass us like this. I'll never come to your country again.'

The police officer was amused. He consulted the petty thieves who confirmed that foreign women had ulterior and sinister motives for every action. Expose the film, they cried.

Then Alison made a dramatic about-turn. Her anger and outrage dissolved into a flood of tears and snot as she remembered her analyst. She buried her face in her hands and wept uncontrollably.

Chika looked perplexed.

Alison wept and shook until her ears turned scarlet. She wept for the Fulani cows, the basket-weavers, the calabash-carvers, and the women with babies on their backs who would all be declared non-existent with one flip of the officer's thumb. They would remain forever shadowy memories of an exotic land.

The officer was visibly disturbed. He had never seen a white woman cry before. 'Madam, madam, don't cry. We are not going to do anything to you.' With that he tucked the camera in its case and held it out to Alison. Soggy tissues in hand, she received it together with her passport and papers.

Alison and Chika stumbled out of the police station.

'Bastard!' muttered Alison, dry-eyed, as Chika opened the car door for her.

Alison had soaked the chickpeas overnight. Her special hummus-and-tahini recipe was yet to be demonstrated before getting to the airport. She got dressed and went into the kitchen for a farewell hug and some more tears. 'Leave some of that rescue-remedy for me,' said Chika, also getting tearful, 'I'll need it.'

louise

She stood in her sunny garden, shovel in hand, tending to her carnations the day I met her. 'Would you like some flowers for your vase?' she asked as she came up to meet me. I hesitantly shut the car door behind me, pulled the *gelle* over my shoulder and shook hands with her—a warm handshake. She wore a pale-blue skirt and a printed blue top to match, her hair was almost all grey, she wore glasses and had the most beautiful and reassuring of smiles. Her living room, as we went inside, reflected her warmth—brown and orange cushions on cosy settees, a fireplace with a rocking chair beside it, roses in a crystal vase in front of the hallway mirror reflecting a million hues, *National Geographic* and *Architectural Digest* in piles along the window-seat, embroidered tapestries of rural Nigerian scenes framing the walls and a pinboard covered with photographs of family and friends. She brought me herbal tea spiced with cinnamon and cloves and walnut cookies. That was the beginning of our friendship.

I expected to be bombarded with a sermon and suitably impressive religious literature. Instead we exchanged recipes and household tips on maintaining a flower garden in the harmattan season.

'There is a bat trapped in those louvres,' she said to me once, pointing to her living-room window. I looked beyond, at the fruit trees laden with oranges, the branches brushing the louvres.

She was a tactile person. Caressing came naturally to her, not only the soft mantle of her words that enveloped you, but her arms seemed ever outstretched to take on the cares of needy women. They sought comfort in her presence when a husband did not come for the night, when the arrival of a young second wife disrupted one's peace of mind or when a child kept one awake at night with malaria or epilepsy. The rose and carnations told a cheerful tale as you cast your eyes about her living room—a glass jar full of candy in coloured wrappers sat on the centre table.

It was so easy to talk to her. You didn't have to choose your words or shape your phrases to impress her. She would have seen through any pretence. She had no formula for friendship or discipleship. As a Zen Buddhist she probably would have been the same person. She told me of the time when in the middle of a bitterly cold New England winter, she had snuggled inside her warm fur coat. Her three-year-old granddaughter had stroked her furry arm, utterly fascinated, and said 'puppy?'. She referred to her pre-retirement days as the 'dark ages' when as a fully qualified and trained nurse she had tended to the sick and lonely for several years.

Whether it was to remove the stain off my ceramic floor tiles, to get a practical recipe for boeuf bourguignon or to stave off my friend's spiritual despair, she was the one that first came to mind. Thursdays became special days when as members of her Transformed Life Study Group, the seven of us gathered round her dining table, she taught us simple faith with childlike trust and eagerness. 'With you I realize,' wrote my friend Nana, 'what it means to have a mother.' She enjoyed her Thursday mornings too, and our company; the pink carnations on the sideboard welcomed us into her dining room. She offered us a range of hot and cold drinks to choose from. We usually settled for her aromatic Russian tea. Our two hours together were rarely interrupted except for the occasional phone call. She was not testy or irritable. 'We are in the middle of Transformed Life,' she would cheerily announce on the telephone, 'come and join us.'

Her enthusiasm was infectious. John was the focal point, the centre of her universe, but only next to God. When she told me she was once afraid that she loved John more than God and had to order her priorities, I believed her.

From where I regularly sat at the dining table, I could see part of her little kitchen, the enamel kettle on the stove, frilly curtains letting in the mid-morning sunshine, little vases on the windowsill with yellow rosebuds in them, and miniature cacti. The kindergarten next door competed with us from time to time, children romping in the yard and shouting at the top of their voices. However turbulent our minds had been before we got there, tempers frayed and nerves on edge, there was a peace that settled over us. We listened to her, prayed, exchanged confidences and reaffirmed each other under her unobtrusive spiritual guidance.

It was not that Louise had all the answers. When all doors seemed closed she just 'felt' with us and waited for a crevice of hope. She knew that Lilian's husband was in prison on trumped-up embezzlement charges. Lilian oscillated between anger and frustration as Louise held her against her bosom and prayed. When Lilian had calmed down sufficiently, she walked her to the bus with a bag of homegrown cabbages, and cookies for the children. Lilian's prison visits became a time of cheerful anticipation—her husband began to respond to her enthusiasm and even talked about the 'future'.

Charity was tormented by nightmares and visitations from previous dabbling in the occult. Louise gave her homely advice on caring for her daughters. The lack of a male child in the family was not a sad comment on her worth as a wife and a woman. Charity slept like a baby at night and put her daytime energies into indoor gardening.

Louise recalled her mother with warmth and tenderness, particularly the time when the family was barely sustaining itself. A piano was not within her mother's financial reach. Yet the little girl lingered in church each Sunday, savouring the music and longing to play the notes herself. 'Dear God,' wrote her mother on a piece of paper. 'We need a piano,' and thrust the folded piece of paper in a crack on the wall near the fireplace.

She continued to write little intimate notes to God as her faith strengthened. Just after Christmas, when the windows rattled on a cold wintry morning, the local daily carried an advertisement: 'Piano in reasonable condition. For sale: $200.' The piano was promptly brought home in a neighbour's pick-up truck. The little girl fingered the notes lovingly. Mother arranged for piano lessons with the church organist in return for some sewing she would undertake to do. Thus began her service to God through the gift of music.

Her intuition startled me. It had never been easy for me to confide in someone. I stewed over my problems, ranted to myself, wept over them in the bathroom and finally accepted my lot with bitterness. But she made me talk—it was her friendly acceptance, her total lack of condemnation. She made me air the little niggling worries that gathered momentum and formed edifices in my mind. The scripture verses came naturally to support her sympathetic counsel.

I had been wary of religious fanatics ever since my charismatic neighbour spoke in tongues and declared me 'born-again' before I had had time to digest his theology. I searched my mind—the catalogue of Christians presented a less than agreeable picture.

The one-armed preacher of the Seventh Day Adventist Church stared at me out of his dark-rimmed glasses. He was like a movie star, I thought, in my eleven-year-old mind. The sleeve of his blue-checked shirt hung loose over the stump of his left arm. I was overcome with pity and admiration for Mr Watts who took it on himself personally to save me. 'Have you accepted Christ as your Saviour?' he inquired earnestly, towering over me. I had in my mind accepted Christ as one of the numerous deities that adorned the walls of my mother's prayer room, incense wafting up and flame flickering in the brass lamp. Then came the Franciscan nuns and priests in the convent school. The early morning mass, the novenas, the Hail Marys, the Latinisms, the holy water and the sign of the cross—these were the life-savers in my adolescent search for significance. I exchanged a set of traditional rituals for these. I wept when Sr Alfrieda took her final vows in the little chapel behind the cloisters. That was the ultimate sacrifice to me.

My husband had been through the routine channels of colonial Christianity and had now arrived at the shores of Ecclesiastes—'a common destiny awaits the righteous and the sinner. So eat and drink and enjoy the fruits of your labour,' he summed up for my benefit. As a child he had accompanied his mother to the local Methodist church, a tumbledown mud-structure that stood beside the railway line, hidden by the tall grass in the rainy season. Here, he chewed on the sugar cane and played amidst the wooden benches as the women prayed and clapped and danced in a frenzy. The European missionary addressed the band of women in English. This was promptly interpreted into a message of doom by the assistant pastor who dramatized it, embellished it, and made the sermon seem twice as long, and threatening. He seemed convinced of imminent disaster.

At forty, as I wavered on the threshold of religious belief, having dismissed ancestral worship and reincarnation to the landscape of memory, my husband dampened my newfound enthusiasm. 'Why don't preachers ever talk to you as mature thinking people?' he asked. 'They always speak down to you as children, exhorting and admonishing.' He alerted me to the unresolved contradictions in the scriptures.

'What is your story?' the pastor asked, looking down at us from the podium. He had just condemned most vehemently the 'adulterers and fornicators' of this world and had told us that his wife had been his best friend for the past twenty-two years. There was no way I could aspire to his status of righteousness. We were going through a sticky patch in our marriage. My husband certainly didn't see me as his best friend nor was he mine, that day. We avoided conflict by not speaking to each other. The rest of the sermon lost its meaning for me.

But Louise—she was a unique person. On Thursday afternoons she had a group of women around the dining table embroidering cushion covers and filling in elaborate cross-stitch patterns of rural landscapes. Nothing set her apart from them except her pale skin, if you cared to notice. There was laughter and merriment and animated Hausa conversation. Her American accent came through occasionally. They called her Mamma.

She painted landscapes and tuned pianos. 'I don't like mystery about houses,' she said, as we flipped through a glossy magazine of home designs. She was not one for dark nooks and corners in architectural layout. That's the sort of person she was, open, frank and transparently honest.

She collected postcards and coffee mugs. On the mahogany chest in the dining room she had a row of mugs from China, Brazil and Burkina Faso. She once gave me a chain made out of newsprint—redundant church weeklies cut up and rolled into beads and threaded to form a chain. Her creativity had no limits. Yet she always gave God the glory. 'That is what I like about being a Christian,' she would say. 'God is full of surprises.' As I drew my blanket tight about me on cold harmattan mornings, I imagined her out there, on the tennis court where she usually walked, prayer journal in hand (as the morning mists lingered on the avocado trees), thinking of and remembering with concern the people of this world.

She was positive and affirmative about everything. We were a close and committed group that depended on each other. The prayer retreat was a moving experience that left us emotionally charged. As we sat in that echoing valley surrounded by jagged rocks looming large above us, we were all stirred to eloquence. She clung to her pink nylon jacket. When she put her hand over my head and prayed, my eyes welled up and hot tears stained my cheeks. The wind howled about us sweeping the very words from her lips. She was going to America a few weeks hence, and I knew I might never see her again.

She established a bond with people through gestures of loving and giving. There was no job description that tailored her activities or limited her generosity. 'When I am sick, I hope you will be around me to nurse me,' she said and smiled.

That smile had a special meaning for me, when the lines gathered round her eyes and there was a conspiratorial gleam about them.

exile

Palms joined together I greeted, hesitant from a safe distance. For a child it was an awkward routine. You got dragged to the living room every time there was a visitor. I joined my palms together tentatively, then went about twisting the curtains that divided the passageway from the living room, or stood on one leg, scratching my left ankle with my right toe until my mother perfunctorily dismissed me from the scene. As a grown woman it was still not easy, a contortion of the limbs that came gracefully to other women, perhaps, but sat uneasily on me. It was drawing attention to oneself. Further, the response could not be predicted. I wasn't much good at the old ritual of prostrating at the feet of elders either. There was the chance, in my case, of clumsily landing at the wrong feet. Moreover, you were never sure who was old enough to merit your going on hands and knees and who wasn't. Never had I been embraced socially though, or attempted an embrace except that once.

In my husband's culture, people habitually put their arms around each other spontaneously, long-lost relatives, friends and born-again Christian sisters. In slow motion, on mental replay, what happened in Mamma's courtyard was my mistake. I had broken a code, acted out of turn in a gathering of elders, as it were. It was a bit like twisting the curtains and scratching my foot in public, except more serious, given the circumstances.

Mamma needed a very good reason to come to the city. And when she came, she complained bitterly about the lights being too bright in the house and the coffee cups too small. Away from the farm and the neighbourhood chit-chat, she was restless. She would walk around the yard and give us all jobs to do: wash the bitter leaf for the soup, slice the green pawpaws and dry them in the sun, shell and sift the melon seeds, and pack all the empty bottles and plastic containers for her to take back to the village. She didn't approve of anyone staying out late, least of all the young women in our household. A niece got told off that she was a 'taxi without a garage', the kind that sought the shade of any tree on the wayside.

Travelling south to the hometown was not a big deal for my husband. He routinely bought potatoes, onions and 'bar-soap' to distribute to the members of the extended family, and returned with yams, plantain bunches and local chickens spilling out of the trunk of his car. But to take a foreign wife and children who were neither here nor there, on a formal visit, it had to be Christmas or a family wedding.

On seeing me, the street urchins called out '*oyinbo*' and ran after the car. It was a six-hour drive on a road that twisted itself round hilly terrain, unfurled through a teak plantation, dropped into a valley with oil palms on one side and a banana grove on the other, and came out on to flat yam country. We were reminded on every trip that my husband's hometown and the country thereabouts produced enough yams to feed the entire continent! Sure enough, as far as the eye could see, green and succulent yam seedlings sprouted and trailed out of mounds of chocolate-brown earth. All along the road farmers sold yams, arranged in pyramids according to size. It was the king of crops in this part of the world.

A major highway stretched from the north of the country to the south, and ran right through the 'hometown'. It seemed like a town of contented people to me, where at midday the women pounded yam in wooden mortars and the men drank freshly tapped palm-wine in open-air bars, and expected nothing from the government. And the cars, buses and lorries thundering past the colonial outpost churned up the fine red dust, splattering the whitewashed houses on either side of the highway, making the town look perpetually red.

Mamma's house was on a little street off the highway, traditional, with a central courtyard and rooms opening into it. If you walked down a lane, on one side of the house, you could enter the courtyard directly. Over the years this had become the centre of social life for the entire extended family and for the neighbourhood as well.

Here, Mamma Ochanya on her way home from the market (a single yam stuffed in a plastic handbag balanced on her head) stopped to greet Mamma and ask if the daughter in Lagos had given birth. Children curtsied and called out a greeting as they rushed past Mamma's courtyard. The village hairdresser, a thin, gaunt woman with her dyes in a basket, wheeled her bicycle past Mamma's courtyard and stopped to ask if Mamma needed 'retouching'. It was here that the village letter-writer had read my husband's letter from overseas, my photograph had been passed around and, amidst muted half tones and whispers, the idea of an *oyinbo* wife had become a reality.

Mamma's bedroom (which also housed a dysfunctional deep freezer and stacks of enamel containers) opened out into the courtyard. Mamma sat at the doorway of her bedroom on a low stool, facing the general entrance. Nothing escaped her eye from this vantage point. Chickens scratched amid the yams, and cassava tubers piled in a corner of the courtyard. Was it on that trip that two women were cleaning out fish in huge enamel basins? With the flick of nimble fingers fish guts spilled out—the sliced fish was washed, piece by piece, with great economy, in the water in the basin and flung into a basket nearby. Beside the covered well in the courtyard, a young cousin sat rinsing dishes in a tub. Another pounded dried okra and herbs in a little wooden mortar. Over our heads a clothesline dangled with wrappers and children's underwear.

This courtyard echoes with women's wails as I recall a young brother's tragic death in a motor accident. Wrappers hitched up and hair bundled in nylon scarves, the women at first sat motionless with their backs to the wall, each nursing a private sorrow. Every now and then they went out into the street to blow their noses, before changing places. Then they wept, sang and sermonized in turn, while others fetched water from the well, cooked, cleaned and served the guests. The family remained an inner circle hushed in their grief. We slept on mats in the courtyard that night, guests and family huddled together under the cold and pale stars. The church choir sang and danced; their bodies moved like lightning in the subdued light of the courtyard. Mamma Onyebe, the soothsayer, sat up in the middle of the night, wrestling with spirits in a hoary prophecy of death. There were stirs and murmurs. Her chant grew louder as one by one the women sat up on their mats, misty figures rocking back and forth muttering the name of Jesus. At daybreak, all ghostly presence dispelled, they gathered in groups fondling babies and reminiscing over previous calamities, their pain blunted by the passage of time.

They seemed an impenetrable wall in the courtyard, strong and resilient, vacillating between idle gossip and homegrown comfort. The Prayer Warriors from the Pentecostal church down the road had taken it upon themselves to use every occasion available for spiritual reinforcement.

'It is like this,' said Aunt Eya. 'When you get on the bus, some people get off at Ikeja, some at Apapa, some at Illupeju. The boy had reached his destination and he got off. If you stay on the bus beyond your destination, there is problem. I hope you get me . . .,' she trailed off.

Another elderly visitor said, 'Sister, I think it's that name you gave your child—Funso, give me for safekeeping—that is the problem. Now, the owner has asked for his property back, who are you to say no? That name . . .' And she clicked her tongue.

The place came alive the day of Brother Anthony's wedding. Trays of pounded yam and *egusi* soup went to and fro, to visitors who sat on wooden benches, stools and bamboo recliners all over the courtyard. The music was loud and children chased each other, ducking in between the food carriers. Mamma made sure there was a big barrel of *kunnu* full to the brim, in the corner of the courtyard. She personally supervised its dispensation, as plastic mugs were dipped into the barrel and jugs refilled for wedding guests.

Patience, my 'co-wife', considers herself something of an alien as well, coming from the eastern part of the country. In her *aso oke*, heavy as a blanket, and stiffly starched head-tie, she herded her children into one of the bedrooms and forced pounded yam into them. She warned them that the wedding would take hours. 'No food there, O!' she said, rolling her eyeballs. Everyone had to be fortified before the church wedding. Patience is the kind who would swear by the Maggi bouillon cube—her soup would not be complete without it. And then this monosodium glutamate had come into the market, wrapped in cellophane and called White Maggi, or Ajinomoto.

'For cleaning bathrooms,' Patience declared. She wasn't going to touch it. She had been part of this family longer than I have, and was in the habit of soliciting privileged information from dubious sources.

My sisters-in-law looked gorgeous in white lace with orange and gold head-ties and *aso oke* shoulder pieces to match. It was obvious from the way they strutted about that they wanted to be set apart as the 'family'.

'See the uniform?' Patience nudged me with her elbow. 'They didn't tell you and me about it, did they?'

A big-bosomed niece walked past, swinging her hips.

'Three months pregnant, they say,' Patience commented, and then changed the story to the parable about casting the first stone.

'See that woman in blue?' Patience continued to gripe. 'That is Brother Solomon's girlfriend. Married man! Hmm . . . you won't believe it! They say he paid to train her.' (Train her in what? Being a monkey in the zoo?)

She grabbed me by the wrist in the courtyard and dragged me into one of the bedrooms—there was going to be trouble at the wedding, she said, haggling over the bride price. 'You and I,' she breathed a sigh of relief, 'are out of it. We'll just be watching.'

Mamma's voice in the courtyard sent us scurrying towards the backyard. There the cooking stones had been arranged and a wood fire was blazing. I took over the frying of the fish. I had never cooked over a wood stove before; the smoke filled my eyes and hair. Sister Agnes had come to the wedding with her Lagos friends, a bunch of army wives with permed hair, imported handbags and shoes with platform heels. They decided to make a salad, which seemed like something they could manage. They diced and chopped a mountain of lettuce, carrots and cucumbers, which would, at the end of the day, have Heinz mayonnaise poured over and blended.

Everything was done without anyone taking charge of the whole operation; the menu seemed to emerge as we boiled, fried and stewed. No one gave orders, but comments were made with varying degrees of authority. 'Too many cucumbers,' said Patience, whisking past. 'Is there salt in the fish?' asked one of the Lagos ladies through the fish haze, and followed it with 'Don't "turn" the fish in the oil. Just leave it to go dry, or it will break up.'

Before long, putting their salad effort aside, the army wives retired to a corner of the courtyard for their tea break, with Tetley teabags and Carnation milk which they produced from their handbags.

I remember now—it was neither a wedding, nor a funeral, or Christmas, that time. We had just returned to the country after two years in Europe and were duty-bound to visit the hometown. The potholes on the highway were worse than before. Purple watercolour mountains loomed in the distance. The yam heaps were there, but fewer, the oil palms and banana groves stood laden with fruit as we had left them. But all along the road, at every village, people had arranged in the place of yams bundles of firewood, ready to be sold. How long would it be before the encroaching desert reached Mamma's hometown?

We arrived in that little red town, hot and tired. Cars heaved, sighed and spluttered down the streets of the red town, spewing thick black smoke from the exhaust. A gaily painted truck trundled past bearing the sign 'No Brain is Idle'. Coming from the land of overfed people, everything looked old and worn, dogs and cats, lean and emaciated. The butterflies in my stomach started flitting madly as we passed the Community Bank, the post office with its paint peeled off and the railway crossing, and headed for Mamma's house. All along the street, it seemed people sawed off trees wherever they found them and whenever they were in need of firewood. Tender shoots grew out of the amputated limbs of *dogon yaro* trees.

I tried to recall the traditional greeting, the clan-title by which Mamma had to be addressed, the genuflection, the stock responses. I would have to reacquaint myself with life in the hometown beyond wearing it as a cameo brooch, reflecting myriad colours from afar. Would there be running water in the taps? Coffee?

As we turned into the narrow street I could see children rushing in to announce our arrival. '*Oyinbo oyoyo*,' they shouted in unison. Mamma, who was on her usual seat in the courtyard, stood up and made her way to the entrance in a stately dance, singing praises to God and clapping. The women around her clapped as well, and joined in the chorus. There was an air of expectancy, a knot at the base of my stomach.

Unknowingly, I entered the courtyard first. Mamma looked much older than when we had left her. Without giving it a thought, I went up with my arms outstretched to embrace her.

She continued the dance movements, elbows bent, feet moving to an internal rhythm, but it was as if she didn't see me. As if I didn't exist. Her eyes were fixed in ecstasy, their gaze went past me to her son and grandchildren coming after me. I had barely touched her when, with one strong elbow, following the rhythms of the dance, she forcefully shoved me aside. Still dancing, she went up and embraced her son and grandchildren, one by one. There was laughter and joy of reunion. So many voices in breathless spasms—'My! How he has grown!' 'Do you still remember our language?' 'Doesn't he look exactly like his father?'

When she finally turned to come towards me, I cowered and froze at her touch. My head reeled in the midst of alien voices, gestures and unfamiliar faces. Their resonance reached me deep within a cavern.

It all happened so quickly, so naturally. The message was conveyed to me, quick and sharp, a message I was not to forget for life. The festivities in the courtyard had only just begun.

The following stories in this collection have previously been published:

'The White Rooster,' *Kunapipi* 14:3, 1992.
'Golden Opportunities,' *Kunapipi* 16:1, 1994.
'Survivor,' *Stand*, 38:1, 1996.
'Exile', *The Picador Book of African Stories*, ed. Stephen Gray (London, Picador: 2000).
'Blessing in Disguise', *The Toronto Review of Contemporary Writing Abroad* 18:3, Summer 2000.
'Jaded Appetites', *Beyond Gold and Other Stories*, ed. David Ker (Makurdi: 2002).

Read more in Penguin

BLUE BLOOD

Uttara Chauhan

'*People associate us former royals with the usual things: images of grandeur—of pomp and splendour, of crowns and coronations . . . They conclude, generally, that to be royalty—even former royalty—is an enviable thing. Well.*'

Peeling back the layers of myth and innuendo surrounding erstwhile royalty in India, the stories in *Blue Blood* explore the lives of individuals who, bereft of power and wealth, must now live as commoners, grappling with the banalities of modern life.

The title story, narrated by an elderly tour guide, unravels the truth behind the tragic fate of Anne Beckford, a European woman who married an Indian maharaja for love. In 'The Birthday', a disinherited gay prince risks disapproval when he returns to his ancestral home for the centennial celebrations of his great-grandfather, a war hero ravaged by Alzheimer's disease. 'The Last King of Portugal', set on the island of Diu, describes the mysterious death of Eduardo Braganza, an Indian-born descendant of the Portuguese royal family. And 'The Search' follows a young woman from Toronto as she embarks on an international quest to find a family heirloom, only to discover a long-kept secret.

With intricate plots and nuanced characters, these eight tales skilfully capture the personal triumphs and tragedies of former royals as they navigate the space between past glory and the reality of the present.

Fiction
Rs 250

Read more in Penguin

EUNUCH PARK
Fifteen Stories of Love and Destruction

Palash Krishna Mehrotra

Among the best I've read in a long time . . .
—Amit Chaudhuri

The most exciting South Asian debut in years
—Aamer Hussein

Palash Krishna Mehrotra writes about prostitutes, cross dressers, murderers, drug addicts, students and stalkers, portraying their perversions and vulnerabilities with equal insight, taking us deep into the dark and seamy soul of India.

Set in the murky underbelly of big cities and small towns, slums and dotcoms, college hostels and rented rooms, *Eunuch Park: Fifteen Stories of Love and Destruction* is a collection like no other. Gritty, grim and depraved, these are candid vignettes of an India most of us are afraid to acknowledge.

Fiction
Rs 250

Read more in Penguin

LUCK

Dhruba Hazarika

Absorbing, spare and often deeply moving . . .
Life in the forests and small towns of Assam
is brought vividly to life by a gifted writer.
— Ruskin Bond

Hazarika is a writer to look out for . . . [for]
the way he manages to squeeze out
maximum emotional impact.
— The Statesman

A hunt goes brutally wrong in the jungles of Karbi Anglong. A young magistrate on a police raid is saved from inhumanity by the sight of a hen and her chicks. A solitary bachelor brings home a pigeon and learns the pain of loving a wild thing. An egret visits a man on a moonlit night. Three schoolboys chance upon a leopard and her kill in the hills outside Guwahati.

In lean, taut prose Dhruba Hazarika writes of moments when men encounter animals and the natural world—often, also the moments when they encounter themselves. These are poignant, memorable stories from a literary imagination of uncommon honesty and sophistication.

Fiction
Rs 199